W9-AWI-975

THE BETRAYERS

in the great Matt Helm suspense series

Don't miss Matt Helm in these bestselling novels of intrigue

"The appearance of a new *Matt Helm* story is always good news. . . ."

Chicago Tribune

"If you have half a dozen thrillers at hand and one of them is by Donald Hamilton, you can either grab it at once or save it for dessert."

New York Herald Tribune

Fawcett Gold Medal Books
by Donald Hamilton:

THE AMBUSHERS   13951-6 $1.50
THE BETRAYERS   14060-1 $1.75
DEATH OF A CITIZEN   14087-3 $1.75
THE DEVASTATORS   Q3512 $1.50
THE INTERLOPERS   13994-8 $1.75
THE INTIMIDATORS   Q3489 $1.50
THE INTRIGUERS   13999-9 $1.75
THE MENACERS   14077-6 $1.75
MURDERERS' ROW   13966-2 $1.50
THE POISONERS   13780-5 $1.50
THE RAVAGERS   13921-2 $1.50
THE REMOVERS   13929-8 $1.50
THE SHADOWERS   14006-7 $1.50
THE SILENCERS   M3000 $.95
THE TERMINATORS   14035-0 $1.75
THE TERRORIZERS   13865-8 $1.75
THE WRECKING CREW   13838-0 $1.50
THE RETALIATORS   13984-0 $1.75

THE
BETRAYERS

Donald Hamilton

FAWCETT GOLD MEDAL • NEW YORK

THE BETRAYERS

© 1966 CBS Publications,
The Consumer Publishing Division of CBS Inc.

ISBN: 0-449-14060-1

Printed in the United States of America

25   24   23   22   21   20   19   18   17   16

THE
BETRAYERS

Chapter One

THERE WERE NO pretty girls with leis to meet me at the Honolulu International Airport, but a greeter-type lady handed me a glass of pineapple juice when I got inside the terminal. I thought this was a comedown from the days when, according to what I'd read, a bushel of flowers and a brown-skinned beauty were just naturally bestowed on every male visitor to the Islands.

If anyone else had any interest in my arrival—and we'd tried to make sure someone would have—he didn't come up and introduce himself. I didn't really expect him to. Mac had made the local situation pretty clear to me after learning where I proposed to take my leave, although he'd stalled a little at first.

"Hawaii?" he'd said, sounding surprised. "Why Hawaii, Eric?"

My real name, if it matters, is Matthew Helm, but we use the code names around that office.

"Because I've never been there, sir," I said. "Because it's a long way off and nobody knows me out there, I hope. Because I feel like lying on a beach for a change, without wondering if the gorgeous creature under the next umbrella is a crafty international spy assigned to lure me to my doom. Any objections, sir? If I'm needed, it's only some five hours by jet to the West Coast."

"Oh, no," he said quickly. "No, of course I have no objections. You have certainly earned a rest. Take it wherever you please." He hesitated. "Will you be going alone?"

"Yes, sir," I said. "You know damn well I'll be going alone, sir. Just me and my conscience."

"Yes, of course. I am very sorry about Claire."

"Sure," I said. "Sorry."

He said, "These things happen, Eric. You did what was necessary." He was silent briefly, and looked up. "I am relieved that you did, of course. I will not deny that I was concerned about your last mission, for a while. It is always unwise for two agents working together to get as emotionally involved with each other as you and Claire had obviously become. I won't deny that I worried lest, influenced by the romantic Riviera background against which you were working, you might let yourself be swayed by sentimental considerations at the last moment."

I said, "Never fear, sir. Within this manly chest beats a heart of pure stone. Sentiment, bah! Now can we stop talking about Claire? She was a nice kid and a good agent, and she did what she had to do, which was die. And I did what I had to do, which was set her up for it. And as a result of our efforts and sacrifices—particularly hers—the operation was a huge success and everybody's happy, at least I hope you are. And now I'm going to Hawaii, formerly known as the Sandwich Islands, and I'm going to practice looking at a beach until I can look at a beach and see nothing but sand. We spent a lot of time on those Riviera beaches, you'll recall, playing bride and groom according to instructions received."

I guess I said that to needle him a little, but he just said calmly, "It worked, did it not, Eric? The opposition took the bait as planned."

"Yes, sir," I said. "It worked just fine. It was just a little hard on the bait, that's all. But I guess that's what bait is for."

"Precisely," he said, and dismissed the subject. "When do you leave for Hawaii?"

"At the end of the week. I couldn't get reservations before then."

Mac was regarding me in a thoughtful way. "You know, of course, that Monk is out there. He's been our senior man in the Pacific area for quite a while."

I grimaced. "I didn't know. Curiosity about other

agents' assignments isn't really encouraged, if you recall, sir, and the Pacific isn't my beat. And I'm not that interested in the Monk. But if I'd known he was out there, I might have picked some other place to go."

Mac said, "Well, it's been a long time since the two of you went into Germany together. That was the Hofbaden job, wasn't it? I seem to remember that you were pretty rough on him."

"Rough, hell," I said. "I'd have killed him if I hadn't needed him, the murderous bastard. It was a perfectly simple job, but he wanted to make a wholesale massacre of it. Is he still getting his kicks from blowing up people in bunches instead of one at a time?"

"Monk's been a good man for us," Mac said evenly. "He has been very effective."

Something in the careful way he put it caught my attention. "Has been?" I said. Then I said quickly, "To hell with it. I don't want to know anything about it, sir. And to hell with the Monk, too. I'm not looking for any more trouble with him, but I've already got my reservations, and I'm damned if I'll change them for him."

"No, of course, not," Mac said. He was still studying me thoughtfully, rather like a cat with an interesting new mouse, but he often looks like that. "Well, have a good time, Eric. Don't forget to stop by the recognition room on your way out."

This was his customary form of dismissal. We're all supposed to spend an hour or two studying the current dossiers whenever we're in Washington, and it's a dull chore, and he's afraid we'll try to dodge it. As I went down to the basement, where the recognition files and projector are located, I told myself that there was no more to the reminder than that, but the memory of his thoughtful expression—and his uncharacteristic curiosity about my vacation plans—stayed with me. I couldn't help wondering if he'd had some cute idea that meant trouble for me. Well, time would tell. He's not a man whose mental processes I try to anticipate.

I couldn't help wondering, however, if he'd had some particular reason for telling me about the Monk. In any case, it wasn't cheerful news, because Monk came under the heading of the kind of unfinished business we normally try not to leave behind us. I mean, it's only on TV that you make bitter enemies in one installment and let them live to raise hell with you in the next. If Monk had been an enemy agent, I'd have shot him dead the instant I had no further use for him, as a simple act of self-preservation. As it was, I'd brought him back to base alive, knowing that I was probably making a mistake, and that it was a mistake the Monk himself would never have made.

Mac was perfectly right: in a technical sense, Monk was a very good man. He was a genius in the field of high explosives, where my own knowledge is less than adequate. The only trouble was, he just loved to see things blow, particularly if the things had people in them. Personally, if I'm assigned to get one man, I like to get that man. This business of demolishing a whole landscape with figures—even enemy figures—just to erase a single individual seems pretty damn inefficient to me. As the agent in charge, I'd had to lean on Monk pretty hard to make him do things my way. He wasn't the man to forget it.

By this time I was sitting in the dark of the projection room, watching the lighted screen display the opposition faces I might come across where I was going. The telephone rang. Smitty, the crippled projectionist, turned his machine to automatic and hobbled off to answer— he'd once made a mistake in the field, so now he had charge down here, a reminder to the rest of us that mistakes can be pretty permanent in our line of work.

He was gone for a while, long enough for the automatic projector to run out of slides. When he returned, he fed it again, and suddenly Monk was looking at me from the screen, older than I remembered him, of course, but with the same hulking shoulders and oddly sensitive, handsome face. I'd never decided whether Mac had picked that code name for him because he was built like a gorilla or because he often wore the expression of a saint, and I'd never asked. There had been more im-

portant things to worry about at the time. I was shown
several recent views of the man and a complete dossier,
the works. Then I was given a rundown on the rest of
our Pacific people, old and new.

I'd started to speak, surprised, when Monk's face first
flashed on the screen, but I'd checked myself. Smitty
knew his business, and obviously he'd received his orders from upstairs. Of course, it was strictly irregular.
Normally we're not allowed to know anybody in the
outfit we don't absolutely have to know, nor are we given
unnecessary information about the agents we do know.
In all the years I'd worked for Mac, I'd never even got
a clear idea of just how many other operatives he had
reporting to him. The only ones I'd recognize were the
ones I'd had occasion to work with, and I was supposed
to do my best to forget those.

For me, a field man, to be briefed on our entire Pacific
apparatus was, I suppose, a great compliment. It meant
that Mac had real faith in me. It was undoubtedly very
unappreciative of me to wish he'd found some other way
to show it, and to wonder just what I'd have to do in
return for this mark of confidence.

From the recognition room I went across the hall to
Hardware and requisitioned a revolver to replace one
that had gone astray over in Europe. I wasn't going to
need it on leave—at least I hoped I wasn't—but the
regulations say we must have one more or less available
always, and I had an uneasy hunch this wasn't the time
to start breaking this particular rule.

The supply man was annoyed with me. "Nowadays
you seem to lose a gun every time you go out, Eric,"
he said. "Yet the record shows that when you were first
with us you used the same .22 automatic for years."

"That was a good gun," I said. "Quiet and accurate.
I liked that little gun. It took care of me, so I took care
of it. But who can get fond of these lumpy, noisy, soul-
less damn .38 caliber blasters you people make us carry
nowadays?"

He said stiffly, "Our ballistics experts have determined

that a cartridge of less power than .38 Special is not suitable for our type of work."

I said, "Who's doing our type of work, me or your ballistics experts? Open up the target range, will you, and lend me a set of earplugs so I can check out this semiportable cannon without being deaf for two days."

He reached into a drawer and brought out a small box, which he opened and held out to me. "Help yourself. Oh, and when you're through here you're supposed to report back upstairs. He wants to see you again before you leave."

It didn't really come as a great surprise. Mac had had time to consider how best to take advantage of my proposed trip. Now he was ready to break the news to me. Well, I'd already gathered that my visit to the paradise of the Pacific wasn't likely to be nearly as restful as I'd planned.

Chapter Two

AS I STOOD IN the airport terminal in Honolulu, on the Island of Oahu, I wasn't really thinking about all this. It was in the back of my mind, of course, but for some reason I was thinking about a girl who'd have enjoyed this trip, restful or not—a girl we'd called Claire, whose real name I'd never learned and probably never would learn now. She was buried in a French cemetery as Winifred Helm, beloved wife of Matthew Helm. On the record, she'd been the victim of an unfortunate traffic accident. With a little local cooperation, you can lose a lot of inconvenient deaths among the highway statistics.

Well, that was ancient history now, or would be as soon as I could make my mind accept it. I finished my fresh pineapple juice, a totally different drink from the sickly-sweet canned stuff you get on the Mainland, and I thanked the greeter-lady for the refreshing experience.

She wasn't bad-looking, but except for the face it was impossible to judge her on points, since she was covered from neck to heels by a long, loose, brightly printed cotton garment with all the sex appeal of a potato sack. While obviously comfortable and indisputably modest, it seemed an odd sort of costume in which to appear in public.

She gave me no secret signs or coded passwords but fluttered off with her tray of juice cups to greet some other passengers from the plane. Nobody signaled me or shot at me as I retrieved my baggage. Nobody threw any knives or kisses my way as I located a taxi, got in, and gave the name of the Waikiki Beach hostelry that had been recommended to me as the kind of quiet, low-pressure place in which a weary man of violence could nurse a broken heart in peace.

After a few blocks, however, I decided that I hadn't escaped entirely unnoticed: we were being followed by a small car of a make I didn't recognize immediately. On the whole it was a relief. If nobody had made a move, I'd have had nothing to do but wait and wonder, but Mac had done his best to insure that my talents wouldn't be wasted.

"I wasn't going to use you on this, Eric," he'd told me on my second visit to his office. "Aside from the fact that you're entitled to a rest, it's a job for which you're poorly qualified. As you say, the Pacific is not your beat. You're unfamiliar with the area, and Monk knows you by sight. However, maybe we can make your apparent disadvantages work for us. In any case, since Monk does know you, if he spots you arriving in Honolulu, as he probably will, he's not likely to believe you're there by chance, even if it's the truth. So for your own protection, if you insist on spending your leave out there, you had better be aware of certain things. . . ."

I couldn't remember insisting on going to Hawaii. All I'd said was that I wouldn't change my plans for one particular guy. I'd have changed them for Mac, but obviously he had no intention of asking me to. He preferred to take me at my word, which left me no out.

Well, I should have known better than to make such a stupid, stiffnecked statement in that office, I reflected, listening to the things he was telling me about the Monk. They didn't surprise me greatly. After all, I'd got to know the guy pretty well at one time—as well as you can get to know a guy you've risked your life with and beat hell out of.

"It is always disturbing when an agent goes bad," Mac said. "Particularly if he's as senior as Monk, he tends to feel himself superior to all rules and laws. After all, he's been breaking them for years in the line of duty."

"Do we know what he's up to?" I asked.

Mac said, "We have conclusive evidence that he's been in contact with Peking."

I said, "That doesn't really prove anything, sir. Hell, I've had contact with Moscow on occasion. There are times when you've got to pretend to be bought. He could have a legitimate explanation."

Mac said dryly, "Your sense of fairness is exemplary, Eric, considering your recorded opinion of the man, which should perhaps have been given more weight than it was."

I said, "I still think he's a bastard, and a dangerous bastard. I'll be happy to shoot him for you, or cut him into little pieces and feed him to the sharks, if they've got sharks out there. But I'm not going to call any man a traitor without proof."

"This has been proved," Mac said. "Monk has sold out. We have checked it carefully. The details don't concern you, but you can take the fact as established."

I don't like facts I have to take as established or details that don't concern me, but there was obviously nothing for me to say but, "Yes, sir."

"As for your original question, no, we do not yet know exactly what he has in mind. Naturally, we must determine that before we take final action. Whatever he's initiated out there under Red Chinese supervision must be stopped. That is as important as dealing with Monk himself. You understand?"

"Yes, sir. Who's on it now?"

"We have one man doing what he can from outside, under the name of Bernard Naguki. If he has occasion to call on you, he will say that there are few seabirds on the Islands, to which you will reply, yes, but the landbirds are very numerous."

I wondered what great brain had dreamed that one up, and how I was supposed to tell the agents from the ornithologists.

I said, "You say Naguki is working on it from outside, sir. Do we have an inside agent, too?"

Mac hesitated. "As a matter of fact, we do. Until we have enough information to act on, Naguki is mainly a distraction, a decoy, as you will be. We do not want Monk to suspect a leak in his own organization. But you will forget I told you this, Eric. It is a very precarious situation, as you can understand, and the agent in question has been promised a free hand and complete anonymity as far as everyone else is concerned. I have given my word on this; I could not have got cooperation otherwise."

I made a wry face. "I love these informers who want to get on the winning side without taking any risks."

Mac said calmly, "I have given my word, Eric."

"Yes, sir."

He showed me his thin, rare smile. "But you haven't, have you? What you learn independently and what you do with what you learn are things for which I cannot be held responsible."

We looked at each other across the desk. I said, straight-faced, "Yes, sir. That clarifies the situation somewhat."

"In theory you will be approached only when you are needed. I will signal that you are coming as soon as I can make contact safely. The identification procedure will be the same."

I nodded. "I gather from what you say that the Monk doesn't know he's been sold, but does he know we're onto him even if he doesn't know how?"

"I'm afraid he's begun to suspect it. That is why I ordered Naguki to get over there and make himself conspicuous, to make it look as if he were the one who had turned up the incriminating evidence."

"That could be rough on Naguki. The Monk can be pretty ruthless."

"Precisely." Mac's voice was unruffled. "That is why I am briefing you, so that you can take Naguki's place if anything should happen to him."

I couldn't help wondering if he had somebody lined up to take my place if anything should happen to me. "Yes, sir," I said. "Thank you very much, sir."

My sarcasm, if that's what it was, was lost on him. He went on smoothly, "You understand, of course, that officially Monk is still a trusted senior operative to whom no breath of suspicion attaches. In fact, the more I think of it, the more I feel that the person under suspicion should be you."

I was careful not to give him the satisfaction of seeing me look startled. "Suspicion of what, sir?"

"Of indiscreet remarks and unstable behavior, disturbing enough to warrant having you suspended and placed under precautionary surveillance. Yes, I think that will work out very well. Disliking you as he does, Monk will want to believe that you are really in disgrace. Very often even a clever man will wind up believing what he wants to believe."

My month's vacation seemed to be receding farther and farther into an unpredictable future. I asked, "Am I permitted to know what I'm supposed to've said indiscreetly?"

"Of course. You were heard to state, among other things, that turning our back on Russia to get involved in Asia is an idiotic error in world strategy, and any lousy second looie who pulled a boner like that on the battlefield would be courtmartialed. I am, of course, quoting you verbatim."

"I see," I said. "Am I also supposed to weep for poor little communist babies fried in dirty capitalist napalm?"

"Not unless you can do it very convincingly. As a cynical and experienced operative, I think you will appear more plausible, at least at first, if you base your arguments strictly on military considerations. Of course, if it becomes necessary to gain the confidence of some particular person, you can let your opinions become gradually more extreme. Or you can back off to safer ground if it seems indicated. It will depend on whom you are trying to impress. Research will provide you with some material that'll give you an idea of the jargon that's being used in discussing the subject."

"Yes, sir," I said. "As you describe them, my original statements don't seem very reprehensible, hardly adequate grounds for suspension and surveillance. So I say that I think Russia is a more dangerous enemy than China, so what?"

Mac said sternly, "For a soldier to question the decisions of his superiors is always reprehensible, Eric. And for an agent to question the policies of his government where he can be overheard is, to say the least, an error in judgment that throws doubt on his professional qualifications."

I said, "Yes, sir. I'm sorry I brought it up, sir."

He wasn't going to let me off that easily. He went on, quoting his own training materials: "An agent is not supposed to attract attention by voicing unpopular opinions, valid or invalid, except as required by a particular assignment. Off duty, an agent is supposed to remain politically inconspicuous, lest he impair his future usefulness. Violation of this principle is sufficient cause for disciplinary action." Mac looked up and spoke in his normal voice again, "I might add that one of the things that first led us to suspect Monk was that some of his people were reported to be publicly taking sides in this debate without being checked or reprimanded in any way."

"I guess I don't have to ask what side they took. What about them in general? Apart from the inside guy we're counting on, whoever he may be, what's the personnel situation out there?"

Mac looked grim. "Unfortunately, because of the distances involved and the special language qualifications required, our Pacific operation has always been more or less autonomous, almost an independent unit within the organization. You will have to assume, in the absence of strong evidence to the contrary, that our Pacific operatives are all loyal primarily to Monk. Most of them were recruited by him, and all of them are accustomed to report to him or through him, rather than directly to me, as in other areas." He moved his shoulders ruefully. "An administrative error, I suppose, but one that could hardly be avoided considering the geographical difficulties."

"Yes, sir," I said. "So he's actually got a little undercover empire at his command. Very handy for a guy with ambitions."

"Yes," Mac said. "Of course, there is a basic flaw in the structure of an empire. Without an emperor it ceases to function."

His voice was soft. I glanced at him and said, "Yes, sir."

"Eric."

"Yes, sir?"

"I have said that Monk is not officially under suspicion. For the sake of everybody concerned, it would be well if his reputation remained unblemished to the very end."

"Yes, sir," I said. "To the very end."

We regarded each other bleakly for a moment. There didn't seem to be any more to say. I turned and left the office.

And now I was riding down the Honolulu waterfront followed by what I'd finally identified as a Japanese Datsun sedan. It was driven by a moonfaced, moustached young man whom I recognized as one of ours—well, of Monk's—code name Francis, currently operating under the alias of Bill Menander. As his crude tailing technique indicated, he was fairly young and inexperienced, or perhaps Monk had instructed him to let me know I was being watched. It would be like the Monk to want to rub it in.

Behind Francis, off and on, was a light-colored Ford a year or two old. I couldn't make up my mind whether

it was part of the parade or just somebody heading for
Waikiki on perfectly innocent business.

Riding through Honolulu in the fading sunlight, I decided that except for some steep and spectacular mountains behind it, apparently of volcanic origin, the city
could easily be mistaken for Los Angeles or Miami
Beach. But you'd never mistake it for the gray German
cities I'd seen with Monk on that long-ago assignment.
We'd both come far since then, but I guess I'd always
been aware that, knowing what I did about him, I'd
made a serious, soft-headed error in bringing the guy
back alive, and that I'd have to set it straight some day.

Chapter Three

I WAS PLEASED by the picturesque, South Seas appearance of the Halekulani Hotel. It was a random
group of unpretentious, rather old-fashioned, cottage-
type buildings with shingled roofs, surrounded by fan-
tastically lush tropical gardens. I'd been grimly resigned
to being filed away by number in a nylon-carpeted
cubicle in one of the usual chrome-plated beach sky-
scrapers, but this place looked reassuringly as if it had
been built to accommodate people rather than credit
cards.

The cheerful boys in blue-and-white sport shirts who
unloaded my gear from the taxi looked as if they'd just
stepped off the nearest surfboard, as did the stocky
brown Hawaiian gent behind the desk who signed me
in, gave me the compass bearings of the beach, bar, and
dining room, and then turned to shuffle through some
mail he produced from a pigeonhole behind him.

"Ah, here we are," he said, handing me an airmail
letter. "I hope you enjoy your stay with us, Mr. Helm.
Aloha, as we say here in Hawaii."

I said, "I thought aloha meant goodbye."

He grinned. "It means hello or goodbye, or just about

anything else you like, as long as it's friendly, Mr. Helm. It is a very useful word."

He passed the key to the bellboy. Following the kid upstairs—apparently I was to be domiciled in the main building—I glanced warily at the envelope I'd been given. I'm not used to getting much private mail. In the business, we don't accumulate many letter-writing friends. We don't even run up many bills under our own names, and I'd arranged to have mine taken care of.

Generally, mail means trouble in code or cipher, but this letter didn't seem to come from an official source. At least I knew of no potential contact masquerading as a firm of San Francisco attorneys. I stuffed it into my pocket as the boy unlocked the door and let me into my room, actually a good-sized suite. Making my arrangements at the last minute, I'd had to take what was available regardless of expense—not a serious financial hardship since, as it turned out, Uncle Sam would be paying the bills.

It was an impressive layout consisting of a bathroom, a small dressing room, and a big bedroom with twin beds, connecting with a smaller sitting room that was actually a screened sunporch with a view of the gardens below. "Lanai" was the local word for this breezy architectural feature, the bellboy informed me. There was a bouquet of unreal-looking, waxy, bright-red flowers on the lanai table, courtesy of the management. Everything looked pleasantly luxurious without being shriekingly new or modern. I thought that with a little effort I might manage to be comfortable here, as long as the Monk let me.

I tipped the bellboy, and when the door had closed behind him I pulled off my jacket and tie, got a flask from my suitcase, found ice and glasses ready on the dresser, and made myself a drink so as not to lose the pleasant edge of what I'd been served on the plane. Crossing the Pacific by air is a rather alcoholic experience unless you're strong enough to fight off the pretty stewardesses, who outnumber you two or three to one. I'm not quite that strong.

I sat down on the edge of the bed to read my letter. It was from a lawyer named Wilson D. Pratt, of the firm of Prescott, Haverford, and Pratt.

My dear Mr. Helm:

As executors of the estate of the late Philip Grant Marner, we have been advised of the tragic death in France of Mrs. Helm, the former Winifred Philippa Marner who, as you are doubtless aware, was one of the two principal legatees under Mr. Marner's will. Please accept our sincere condolences.

We would appreciate your contacting us at your earliest convenience.

Sincerely,
W. D. Pratt

I took a drink from my glass, but it didn't help much. The message still made no sense to me. What confused me, I guess, was the fact that I'd used the matrimonial cover several times in my career as an agent; I'd even had a real wife once. Her maiden name had not been Marner, and we'd been divorced years ago, but it took a second reading of the letter with its reference to France before I realized that this communication did not refer to her, but to my latest pseudo-bride, the one I'd known by the code name Claire.

Winifred Philippa Marner, I thought. Philippa, for God's sake! No wonder she'd never told me her real name, although she'd used the Winifred in playing her honeymoon role. And now some San Francisco legal brains wanted to make me rich, maybe, just because we'd signed a few European hotel registers as man and wife. I thought this was a careless assumption for trained lawyers to make, but then, maybe the estate involved didn't amount to enough to make them careful.

If it did, I reflected, it was a pity they hadn't picked on a man with more larceny in his soul, a man who'd have given them a run for their money—well, for Mr. Philip Grant Marner's money. All kinds of interesting possibilities went through my mind. A little fraud wouldn't be difficult for a man with my training and experience.

I sighed regretfully and, being fundamentally honest, at least where money is concerned, I stuck the letter into a hotel envelope with a note addressed to Mac, through channels, asking him to get these people off my neck. Then I sat for a moment debating with myself whether or not, if the letter were intercepted, this action would seem consistent with my cover as an agent being disciplined for shooting off his mouth irresponsibly.

I decided that such an agent would indeed be careful to appear scrupulously honest, and I went downstairs to buy an airmail stamp and find a mailbox. When I got back to my room, the phone was ringing. I picked it up. There was no sound for a moment except the sound of the wires. Then I heard a man groan with sudden, unbearable pain.

"Hello," I said. "Hello, who's there?"

A rich baritone voice I recognized from years ago said, "Helm? Your friend Naguki wants to speak to you . . . . Speak to the man, Bernard!"

I heard another quick gasp of pain. I said irritably, "Go peddle your practical jokes somewhere else, wise guy. I don't know anybody named Naguki. Goodbye!"

I slammed down the receiver. The flask of bourbon was still standing on the dresser. It seemed like a good idea, and then it didn't. I mean, I like a drink when I want to relax, but these were hardly the circumstances for quiet relaxation. The phone rang again, as I'd expected it to. I gave it a little time to jangle before I picked it up.

"Eric?" It was the same voice.

I said, "All right, funny fellow, now tell me who you are and where you got hold of *that* name."

"This is Monk, Eric. Remember the Monk? Remember Hofbaden?"

I said, "For God's sake! Good old Monk! I thought you'd bit yourself and died of rabies years ago. What the hell are you doing on this Pacific rock?"

"Watching you, Eric. Orders. You've been a bad boy, it seems. You always did talk too much."

I said, "Well, I'll tell you, I thought I was in a democracy, Monk. Free speech and all that jazz. My mistake. I won't make it again, so don't get your hopes up." He didn't speak, and after a moment I went on, "So Washington's ordered you to keep an eye on me? Come to think of it, I did notice an incompetent jerk in a motorized roller skate tailing me from the airport. So what else is new?"

"You're sure you don't know anybody named Naguki, Eric?"

Obviously I didn't know anybody named Naguki. I couldn't know anybody named Naguki. If I did know somebody named Naguki—if I had any interest whatever in a man by that name—my flimsy cover story was destroyed, and I was no longer just a suspended agent killing time in Hawaii. This was, of course, exactly what Monk was trying to force me to admit.

I said, "Go to hell. I don't know anybody in Honolulu but that ex-Olympic character, Duke Kahanamoku —at least I saw his picture once, somewhere. Don't try to frame anything on me, amigo. All I did was talk out of turn. Don't try to build it into something big. I'll stand for the surveillance bit because you're doing it under orders, but don't dream up any frills of your own, like persuading some lousy little enemy errand boy to swear I sold him state secrets. I know you, Monk, and you know me, so don't try it. Don't even think it. Now, what's this Naguki routine?"

"If you don't know him, what do you care?"

I said, "For Christ's sake, if you've got something to say, say it. If you don't, get off the damn line and let me go to bed. It's been a long day and airplanes make me tired."

Monk's voice said heavily, "If you don't know Naguki, I guess you don't mind if we kill him a little."

I said, "Hell, draw and quarter him if you like. He's all yours. I give you Naguki, whoever he may be. No charge. Now can I go to sleep?"

Monk said nothing. He just cut the connection. I replaced the phone gently in its cradle and looked at myself in the mirror of the dresser across the room, but that was a mistake. The guy in the glass looked like a cold-blooded son-of-a-bitch, the kind of callous louse who'd sacrifice a man's life without turning a hair. I told myself that nothing I could have said would have helped Naguki once the Monk decided to grab him. It was probably the truth but it didn't make me feel any better.

I went to bed. After a while I even went to sleep, to awaken suddenly at the sound of somebody nearby crying out a shrill warning. I went into the standard surprised-in-bed routine without stopping to think—if you think about it you often don't survive to do it—and wound up on the rug six feet away, gun in hand, facing in the direction from which the noise had come. I was surprised to discover that it was morning. There was nobody in sight.

I had closed the lanai shutters before turning in, since I don't like sleeping in full view of the outdoors. Why make it easy for a guy with a rifle and telescopic sight? Nothing moved, inside or out. Nobody spoke or screamed. I rose cautiously and backed away and inspected the bathroom and dressing room. Having made sure no danger lurked behind me, I returned to the bedroom and stood there, frowning. Everything was very quiet; then the sharp, hysterical cry that had awakened me came again.

I strode across the porch and yanked back the shutters and looked out from my second-story vantage at a couple of birds about the size of starlings on the shingled roof of the bungalow across the way. They were having a hell of an argument. I grimaced, wondering if perhaps I really needed the vacation I wasn't going to get. I went back to the bedroom dresser and leafed through a pamphlet I'd brought with me and identified the little feathered squabblers as mynah birds. While I was at it, waiting for my circulatory and nervous systems to return to normal, I looked up the unlikely-looking red flower on the table: anthurium.

My watch read barely six-thirty, local time, but I didn't feel sleepy enough to get back into bed. Instead I shed my pajamas, dug out swim trunks and sandals, put them on, and grabbed a towel. When I got down to the beach, I had it all to myself. A large outrigger canoe with the hotel's name on it was drawn up on the sand. The water was blue and clear. The slow waves rolling up to the shore didn't look very big, but half a mile out an occasional one would break into white foam as it stumbled over a reef or shelf out there.

Leaving my sandals and towel on the stone sea wall, I walked out onto the sand and looked around. It was my first real view of Waikiki Beach. If I'd had any childish illusions about the place, they'd have died right there. If you're still dreaming of a long, curving strip of white sand shaded by tall tropical palm trees, forget it. There are a few palms, to be sure, but what you'll find is a long, curving strip of white sand shaded mainly by tall luxury hotels. Even the frowning mass of Diamond Head, the great rock guarding the eastern end of the Bay, hasn't escaped the promoters. Right at the tip, like pimples on Oahu's aristocratic nose, are several monstrous complexes of glass and concrete at least a dozen stories high.

Well, I have no doubt that some financial genius has great plans for filling in the Grand Canyon to make a nice level spot for a tourist resort. The fact that the tourists will then have no view left to look at has been taken into consideration: there'll be a swell eighteen-hole golf course instead.

I guess I was a little disappointed, after all. I told myself, what the hell, I'd known I wasn't coming to a desert island, why should I be surprised that people had built houses on it? I waded into the water, a little chilly at that hour of the morning, and swam out a distance but discovered that I could still touch bottom. Out here, however, it was no longer sand but weeds and coral, nothing you'd care to walk around on barefoot. Not knowing what kind of tropical sea monsters might lurk in the crevices, I paddled hastily back to where I could see what I was stepping on.

After getting to my feet in the shallows, I started to wade shoreward and stopped abruptly. A slender, sun-burned, blonde girl in a scanty white bikini was just coming down to the beach, balancing a red-and-white surfboard on her head. Considering that the board was eight or ten feet long, a couple of feet wide, and probably weighed well over thirty pounds, this was quite a sight in itself, but it wasn't the athletic trick that had startled me. For a moment I'd thought there was something familiar about the approaching figure. I mean, let's face it, Claire had worn a white bikini on occasion.

It wasn't Claire, of course. Claire was dead half a world away, and this was a taller girl with a rangier build. She was just as brown as the girl I'd known in Europe, but her streaky blonde hair was darker—more like light brown hair bleached by the sun—and longer, reaching well down her shoulders. Claire's had been quite short, just a light silvery cap.

As she passed me, the strange girl gave me an impersonal little smile from under the board: just a friendly early riser greeting a kindred spirit. She stopped beyond me to launch her gaudy plank, and straightened up to give a hitch to the bottom of her bikini, or perhaps just to reassure herself that she hadn't misplaced the essential scrap of cloth somewhere. She posed there briefly, breathing the fresh morning air, slowly running her fingers through her uncovered hair, pushing it back from her face.

On the beach, you can tell a lot about a girl by the way she treats her hair. If she comes down to the shore all ratted and lacquered and paddles around in shallow water like a stiff-necked turtle, obviously thinking of nothing but keeping the precious stuff dry, you might as well forget about her. You aren't man enough to get her mind off her coiffure. Nobody is.

If she takes the bathing-cap route and really swims, there's hope for her, but she's either incurably optimistic or not very bright, since the cap hasn't been invented yet that'll keep all water out. But if she just dives in and lets her hairdo wash where it will, you'd better grab her quick before some smart guy beats you to her. She may look a little stringy come evening, but she'll probably be worth it. At least she knows there are more important things in the world than hair.

I watched the blonde girl throw herself onto the surfboard and paddle out to sea with strong simultaneous strokes of her brown arms. The contrast between soft round girl and hard flat board was very intriguing. When a wave splashed over her, it didn't bother her a bit. Obviously she'd come to the water to get wet, hair and all. Obviously also, she was thinking of nothing but getting out to where the big ones were breaking. The fact that a man was watching her couldn't have concerned her less. Obviously.

I sighed and turned away to get my towel and sandals. Under other circumstances, having had such a nice show put on for me, I might have done something impulsive like trying to scare up a beach boy to rent me a surfboard. Not that I knew how to work one, but that wouldn't matter. My early-morning seasprite would be glad of the excuse to teach me, I was fairly sure.

Please understand, I don't normally figure every blonde on the beach is posing just for me, even when she does the fingers-through-the-hair bit and there's nobody around but the two of us. Girls do scratch their heads upon occasion, just like everybody else, and it doesn't necessarily mean a thing, even when it's accompanied by the deep-breathing, isn't-it-a-glorious-morning act.

However, this wasn't a normal situation. I'd been right in thinking there was something familiar about the girl. She wasn't Claire, but I'd seen her picture recently on the screen in the recognition room in the basement of a certain house in Washington, D.C. It had taken me a little while to locate the memory, but I had it now; code name Jill, station Pacific, one of our more promising young recruits in this operational area—that is to say, one of the Monk's more promising young recruits.

It could be just coincidence that she'd picked this morning and this hotel for her pre-breakfast date with the breakers, but I didn't believe it for a moment. Nor did I think I'd have to go to a lot of trouble to make her acquaintance. In fact, I had a hunch I couldn't lose her if I tried.

Chapter Four

NAGUKI HAD MADE the morning papers. Breakfasting on the terrace outside the hotel's dining room, I read about the accident, which had occurred on the Pali, wherever that might be. Apparently I wasn't the only agent who knew how to put the traffic statistics to good use.

There was a picture of the blanket-covered body beside the twisted wreckage of what had been a light Ford sedan a year or two old. It could have been the second car that had tailed me from the airport yesterday. Maybe, feeling Monk closing in on him, Naguki had been trying to make contact with me. If so, he hadn't helped my situation any more than I'd helped his.

In spite of what I knew of the Monk, I was a little surprised, not at the murder—that wasn't unexpected—but at the way he'd boldly signed his name to it by his call to me. Of course, he had been trying to get me to betray myself, but still it indicated that he felt safe and powerful out here, almost invulnerable. Well, he'd always had delusions of grandeur.

"Miss, what's the Pali?" I asked the waitress.

"Pali is cliff or precipice, sir," she said. "Up there in the mountains. On the other side is very steep, the Pali. Also, the highway, very steep, the Pali Drive. Goes to windward side of island. More coffee, please?"

"Thanks," I said, wondering if she were Japanese, Chinese, Hawaiian, or a little of each. It was hard to tell. Anyway, she was a pretty, friendly girl with a nice smile, and she undoubtedly considered herself American, just as Amercian as a guy who'd called himself Bernard Naguki, or for that matter, a character named Matthew Helm. . . .

Afterward, I checked for mail at the desk and found a note from the management inviting me to a hotel-sponsored cocktail party that evening. Reading this, I laid a small bet with myself that I knew where our girl Jill would make her next move. It would save her from having to pull some corny meet-cute stunt like dropping a glove or hanky or surfboard at my feet. You can get acquainted with anybody at a cocktail party and make it look quite natural.

In any event, the initiative was obviously in the hands of the opposition for the time being. There was nothing for me to do but play tourist, so I looked up the phone number of a car-rental place. They sent a small bus to transport me to their office where, for very little money, I was provided with a crippled French Simca that could barely fight its way out into the street. I let its dying struggles carry it back onto the lot and traded it for a British Sprite at twice the rental—but at least the two-seater gave a healthy roar when I tickled it with my foot.

Also it provided me with an excuse to do some moderately progressive driving: you don't rent a sports car to stand still in traffic. Our boy Francis, alias Bill Menander, was back on the job, and I took sadistic pleasure in running him around Honolulu for most of the day, at speeds that had his little Datsun crying for help.

We saw the aquarium where a porpoise jumped through a hoop and got everybody wet and the botanical gardens where orchids grew like weeds. We spent a good deal of time in various historical museums, making a study of Hawaiian royalty. The first five kings were easy, they were all named Kamehameha. After that they started showing individuality, and I lost track of them, but I was careful not to let Francis lose track of me. He escorted me back to the hotel in time for me to change for cocktails: the invitation had specified jacket and tie.

Fully dressed according to specifications, I wandered into the party, given on a terrace covered by a trellis of giant vines in lieu of a roof or awning. I was passed from hand to hand through the receiving line and introduced to some people from New York who were no more interested in me than I was in them, but I saw Jill across the room with orchids in the long blonde hair that hung loose down her back, very striking and, in spite of her morning's swim, not stringy at all.

I was aware when she broke away from her companions, and I turned my back so she could have the satisfaction of sneaking up on me from behind. The stout woman in front of me, in a gaudy new Hawaiian garment quite similar to that worn by the pineapple-juice lady at the airport, was telling me all about crossing the Pacific on the liner *Lurline*. It sounded great if you liked organized fun on shipboard.

Then there were footsteps behind me and the voice of a woman on the hotel staff saying to somebody, "I'm sure you'll have a lot in common. Mr. Helm is from Washington, too."

I turned with my face ready to recognize Jill and my voice ready to make some reference to our early-morning encounter—why make it hard for the girl?—but it wasn't Jill. Jill was standing some distance away with a frustrated look on her pretty face. In front of me, smiling in a bored and world-weary way, stood a very handsome dark-haired woman wearing dark glasses that made her look like a movie star incognito. I'd never seen her before, even in photographs.

I was sure of this. She wasn't anybody you'd forget if you'd seen her once. The New Yorkers were being led away to meet some other fascinating people, leaving me alone with her. I didn't figure I'd lost anything by the trade, and Jill could wait.

I flagged down a boy with a pitcher of the rum punch that was going around, but, as I should have guessed from her aloof—not to say snooty—appearance, my new companion couldn't drink from the common pot. She had to have Scotch, and a particular brand of Scotch at that. We retired to the bar that had been set up in a corner of the terrace for the hard-to-please.

When her glass had been properly replenished, she made a small gesture of raising it to me, drank, and nodded approvingly. We stood there for a while in silence: two strangers forced into each other's company with nothing much to say. The lady's attitude made it clear that she didn't really give a damn whether she talked with me or not. As for me, after years of getting acquainted with people for devious purposes, I find it difficult to do the social bit for its own sake.

At last I said, "I'm sorry, but I didn't catch your name."

"McLain," she said. "Isobel McLain."

I glanced at her left hand. "Mrs. Isobel McLain?"

She smiled briefly. "Yes. Mrs. Kenneth McLain, to be exact."

"My name's Helm, Matthew Helm," I said.

"Yes," she said.

"Have you been in the Islands long, Mrs. McLain?"

Well, you can requisition a few yards of that dialogue from stock and cut it to fit. She hadn't been in the Islands long. In fact, she'd only arrived a couple of days ago. She smiled again and gestured toward her smart, sleeveless black cocktail dress.

"Not long enough to go native, Mr. Helm, as you can see. I'm still breaking the rules by wearing real clothes. They'll probably throw me out of the hotel if I don't buy a muu-muu pretty soon, but these primitive costumes leave me cold."

I had a hunch that a lot of things and people left Mrs. McLain cold, but somehow she made it seem like a challenge. The implication was that, for a very few special things and people, she could be quite warm indeed, and that it was very much worth an effort to find out if you were one of the favored few.

She was really a strikingly good-looking woman, particularly in that company. I mean, at least half the ladies present, Jill included, were sporting the bright native dresses. They apparently came in all conceivable variations of the basic Mother Hubbard theme: long and short, tight and loose, plain and flowered. And while the style isn't unattractive, it doesn't make a woman look particularly well-dressed, at least not to my conservative Mainland eyes. I am also unalterably opposed to bare legs and sandals under dress-up conditions. Pardon me for being stuffy, but if the rules require me to put on coat and tie, the women can damn well struggle into stockings and high heels. Besides, they look prettier that way.

Against that background of shapelessly fluttering prints, Isobel McLain looked unique and priceless in her unobtrusively well-fitting black dress. She gave the impression of being fairly tall, but that was only an illusion, I discovered, looking down at her from my six-feet-four. Without her heels, she'd have been a full foot shorter. Her proportions were attractive, decidedly feminine without being vulgarly spectacular. Her hair was dark brown, done in a smooth, restrained bubble with the ends tucked in, one of the nicer styles evolved from those giant bird's-nest hairdos of a few seasons back.

Her features were regular, her teeth were good, her skin was good, her posture was good, and you could say the same of a thousand women you'd never turn to look at twice. The simple fact was that she was a knockout, at least in the adult division. A man whose taste ran exclusively to leggy, breathless juveniles might not have been as impressed as I was. I put her age between thirty and thirty-five, although she could have passed for less.

I asked, "Is your husband here, Mrs. McLain?"

She shook her head. "No. Kenneth and I are taking separate vacations this year. He finds it restful to watch dice bounce around a table. Or horses run around a track. Or roulette wheels just go around and around and around." She shrugged. "Unfortunately, I don't. And after a while one gets tired of pretending, don't you know?"

A faint uneasiness made me look at her more sharply; she'd said a little too much in answer to a simple question. I mean, the cool, reserved, bored lady she was supposed to be would hardly have let a perfect stranger so far into her private life so soon.

Or maybe she would, away from home with a couple of Scotches inside her—I noticed she'd already set her glass back on the bar for another refill. Still, it was a jarring note, a reminder that in our world of deceit and intrigue nothing was necessarily what it seemed, not even an attractive woman. Particularly not an attractive woman.

"Do I understand that you live in Washington, D.C., Mrs. McLain?" I asked, and we went on from there to discuss the nation's capital and its dreadful summer climate.

I set a couple of casual traps for her—I'd brought up the subject for that purpose—but they caught nothing. Whether or not she actually lived there, she knew the city. She got out of me that I was an underpaid government employee blowing my savings on an extravagant vacation, and we played the do-you-know-Joe game half-heartedly. Neither of us was greatly surprised to discover that, apart from a couple of headwaiters, we had no Washington friends or acquaintances in common. That pretty well finished the supply of cocktail-party conversation on both sides, and the silence was getting awkward when the industrious hotel hostess broke in on us again.

"Here's somebody who insists on meeting you, Mr. Helm. She says that anybody who gets up at dawn to go swimming must be worth knowing."

Our girl in Honolulu had made it at last.

Chapter Five

AS I TURNED TO Jill, introduced as Miss Darnley, I was aware of Isobel McLain being led away in invisible chains. Perhaps it was just as well. I hadn't really been making a red-hot impression there, or if I had, the lady had concealed it bravely.

Jill, alias Miss Darnley, was obviously going to be a different proposition. Her eager expression said she was just waiting to be impressed by me, no matter how stupid and boring I turned out to be.

I noticed that she was dutifully drinking the rum punch, and she seemed to be impersonating, as far as her fair complexion would permit, a cute Hawaiian maiden just converted to modesty and Christianity, in a flowing, flowered muu-muu thing that reached the floor. In addition to the orchids in her hair she had an orchid lei around her neck. This sounds pretty fancy and expensive, I guess, but as I've already intimated, in Hawaii orchids grow like dandelions back home.

I said, "Goody, it's the little girl with the big board. How was the surfing this morning, Miss Darnley?"

"Not very good. We had to wait forever between sets."

"Sets, like in tennis?" I asked.

She laughed. "Big waves come in sets, or groups, of half a dozen or more, Mr. Helm. There'll be a long calm spell when you just sit on the board waiting, and then somebody yells 'outside' and you see the first wave of a set humping up against the horizon. Then you paddle like hell to where you figure the break is coming. Generally you let the first few waves of a set go by, hoping for one big enough to give you a good ride. That's in little summer surf like here off Waikiki. In big winter surf, like off Sunset Beach—that's down at the other end of Oahu—you've got to be careful you don't catch one too big for you to handle and get wiped out."

She was pretty tense, now that she'd finally reached me, and she rattled off this lecture a little too fast, like a kid trying to show off before a grownup—or maybe I wasn't being quite fair. Maybe she'd have seemed to be acting quite naturally if I hadn't known who she was and guessed approximately what she was up to.

"Wiped out," I said, dryly. "Sets. Outside. Why, it's a foreign language."

She flushed slightly. "I gather you're not a surfer, Mr.

Helm." She gave me a cool, appraising glance. "Well, it's not a middle-aged pastime, I guess."

I grinned. "Yes, little girl," I said. "Grandpa's rheumatiz do trouble him something fierce."

She laughed. Having insulted each other, we were now friends. She said, smiling, "You asked for it, being so stuffy. All sports have their jargon. And actually, they're mostly all kids out there; they even treat me as if I were an old lady."

"Fancy that," I said. "A mere infant like you? But it seems odd. You'd think that all these plush hotels, with an interesting sport growing right in their front yards, so to speak, would make a big effort to sell it to the tourists old enough to have a little dough to throw around."

"Well, surfing is fairly strenuous and just a bit dangerous."

"So's skiing," I said. "And look how they're cashing in on that back home. . . . What's the matter?"

"The mix-'em-up lady is heading back our way. I don't really want to meet any more enchanting people, do you?"

It was nicely done. Now that we'd found each other, she was suggesting, we didn't need anybody else. Any man would have been proud to have an attractive blonde so attach herself to him, even a blonde wearing something that, stylewise, resembled nothing so much as my grandmother's winter nightgown. Of course the orchids helped. I put out of my mind the fact that she was undoubtedly acting strictly according to instructions—Monk's instructions—and I let myself expand visibly at the implied flattery.

I said, "Well, I was getting kind of tired of the social whirl myself, Miss Darnley. I suppose we could slip out between those bushes and find sanctuary over there at the open-air bar or whatever they call it. What do you say?"

"I say that would be very nice, Mr. Helm."

She set her glass aside, took my arm, and gathered up her voluminous garment with her free hand, displaying rudimentary sandals and a discreet amount of slim brown legs. Shortly we were being seated under a giant tree on the seaside terrace in front of the bar or cocktail lounge, a rustic building that had been shuttered that morning but was now exposed to the breezes from several directions, more a pavilion than a house.

Near us under the big tree, a dark, beautiful, but rather buxom young lady in a long, heavy, red brocade gown was doing a slow hula to the accompaniment of a ukelele, a steel guitar, a string bass, and an electrified instrument that looked like an autoharp on legs. I was rather startled to see that, below the regal gown, the lovely dancer's feet were bare. Beyond the band, far out at sea, a large ship was steaming slowly toward Honolulu harbor in the pinkish glow of the setting sun.

I said, "Look, there's a ship out there. Would that be the famous *Lurline* people have been telling me about?"

Jill didn't turn her head. "No, the *Lurline* arrives on Saturdays, in the morning and it's quite an occasion. You'll have to see it. All the boats and catamarans go out to meet her. It's a real nautical traffic jam, usually, with water skiers showing off and boys diving for coins and everybody yelling aloha. Real corny but kind of fun." She glanced over her shoulder. "There's supposed to be a transport ship due with troops for the Far East. Some of them stop off here. That must be it." She smiled at me. "And you weren't really looking at any ship, Mr. Helm."

I grinned. "Hula me no hulas. I've seen a girl wiggle her hips before." A waitress was hovering over us, wanting our orders. I said to Jill, "You name it, Miss Darnley. What goes with rum?"

"More rum, of course," she said, and looked up at the waitress. "Two Mai Tais, please. . . . I think you'll like this drink, Mr. Helm."

"If it's got alcohol in it, I generally do," I said, and went on casually, "What the hell are those birds? They look like doves, but they act like sparrows."

Jill glanced at the birds picking up crumbs under the tables. "They are doves," she said. "We have two kinds, big ones and little ones. But you really should watch this dance, Mr. Helm. It's the real hula, not the grass-skirt shimmy all tourists seem to expect when they come to the Islands. Look at her hands. Aren't they graceful?"

"Hands? What hands?" I said. "Oh, you mean the *hands*. Oh, sure. Very graceful."

Jill laughed at my clowning, and I laughed with her, and we were off birds as quickly as we'd got on them. What it amounted to was that I'd given her an opening for the seabird-landbird password and she'd let it go by. This meant either that she wasn't the inside agent Mac had spoken of, or that she wasn't ready to reveal herself yet. Well, I hadn't really expected it to be that easy.

I asked, "Do you live here on Oahu, Miss Darnley?"

"I'd hardly be staying at a hotel if I did," she said. "Oahu isn't so big that you can't get home at night, wherever you are. No, I live in Hilo. That's on the island of Hawaii, what we call the Big Island, the one with the volcano. Well, they're all volcanic, of course, but our volcano really works, from time to time." She smiled. "And my name is Jill, Mr. Helm."

"Jill Darnley," I said. "Very nice. I'm Matt. How long are you staying in Honolulu, Jill?"

"Oh, a week or so. It depends. Did you say you knew something about skiing, Mr. Helm? . . . I mean, Matt."

"I didn't say, but I do. A little. Why?"

"Well, if you can ski, you'd probably have very little trouble with a surfboard. I mean, it's all a question of balance. And if you're getting up early again tomorrow, well, I could promote another board and show you. . . . It's really a fantastic sport. Out of this world. There's nothing quite like it. I mean, of course, if you want to."

I said, "Sure, but I hope you're not hinting that you want to be rid of me until tomorrow morning."

She said very quickly that of course she wasn't, then the Mai Tais arrived. The recommended drink turned out to consist of heroic quantities of rum in a large glass into which had been inserted some ice, a stick of fresh pineapple, and so help me, an orchid. Jill told me that Mai Tais were originally concocted with a wicked local brew called *okolehao,* distilled from the fermented root of the *ti* plant, the same useful plant that provided the leaves for the famous grass skirts. However, oke, as it was called, was such violent stuff that it had been replaced by rum for tourist consumption, said Jill.

She was really a very informative girl. By the time we'd finished our Mai Tais at the hotel and a couple more rounds with dinner at Duke Kahanamoku's night club and had sat through the floor show there—with all the MC's local references explained to me by my blonde companion—I was practically a native Hawaiian myself. It was well after eleven when we got back to the Halekulani. We stopped in the lobby and looked at each other. There was an awkward little pause.

I cleared my throat and said, "How about a nightcap? I haven't any oke, but I've got a Mainland drink you may find tasty. We distill it from grain and call it bourbon."

She laughed. "Are you making fun of me, Matt? Have I been talking too much like a tour guide?" I didn't say anything. She stopped smiling and looked down and blushed a little, which showed promise. A kid who can blush on demand will go a long way in our trade, if she survives. "Well," she said. "Well, all right. Just a quick one."

We didn't say anything going up the stairs, but she slipped a hand under my arm, ostensibly for support. Maybe she really needed it. We'd both absorbed respectable amounts of rum during the course of the evening.

We stopped at my door, and she leaned against me sleepily while I unlocked it. Normally I'd have taken a precaution or two, entering the place again after having been out of it so long, but precautions weren't really feasible with the girl practically crawling into my pocket. They would have been wasted, anyway. No booby traps blew as we went inside; no hidden assassins leaped out at us.

I paused to lock the door. Jill detached herself from me and went on through the lanai into the bedroom part of the suite. When I turned to look at her, she was standing there, waiting, doing once more for me the lazy, provocative business of pushing back her long hair with both hands.

"I . . . I don't really want another drink, Matt," she said, letting her hands fall as she watched me approach.

"I didn't think you did," I said, stopping in front of her. "But a man's got to say something, doesn't he?"

"I suppose so." She smiled slowly. "Now help me out of this ridiculous garment. . . . Or maybe you'd better kiss me first."

"Sure."

I kissed her. She came breathlessly alive in my arms; it was an interesting performance, as a display of technique. I mean, she was putting on a pretty good show for an inexperienced kid, and suddenly I was disgusted with both of us and our phony passion.

She was too busy playing Jezebel to notice. She sighed and freed herself quickly, turned away, and pulled her lei off over her head and tossed it onto a nearby chair. The lose muu-muu dress dropped to the floor. She got rid of brassiere, panties, and sandals in what seemed like a single graceful motion, and swung back to face me expectantly.

I took a step backward. "Very good, Jill," I said. "Oh, very good indeed. Tell the Monk I said you did that extremely well." Her face turned pale. I said harshly, "Now you can get dressed again before you catch cold. I'm a big boy and I don't talk in my sleep. Seduction is for kids, honey, and I'm surprised the Monk would have you try it on an old hand like me. He must be slipping."

There was a little silence. I had to hand it to her, she didn't try any indignant, useless protests. She didn't try to persuade me she didn't know anybody called Monk and I was making a terrible mistake. She didn't say anything at all.

She just licked her lips and bent down to pick up her clothes and turned away from me again to put them back on. She took time to do it right, getting all the hooks and snaps and zippers fastened properly. Then she walked straight to the door and stopped, and looked back over her shoulder, speaking at last:

"That was . . . just a bit cruel, wasn't it, Matt? You didn't have to do it like that."

I stared at her for a moment, as if not quite believing what I'd heard. Then I walked quickly across the room and took her by the arm and swung her against the wall, holding her there.

"Cruel, baby?" I said savagely, leaning close to her. "Who are you to talk about cruel? Do you know where I was a month ago? I was in Europe, working with a girl. She was sunburned and nice-looking, like you. She was blonde, like you. She had blue eyes, like you. She wore a white bikini, just like you. And if you think the resemblances are coincidental, you're out of your cotton-picking mind. You were selected for this crummy job, Jill, because Agent Eric is supposed to have a weakness for tanned blondes; because the girl, I'm talking about died over there and somebody had the cute notion I'd be just about ready for a replacement. Don't talk cruel to me, sweetheart. Just get the hell out of here."

She didn't move at once. She whispered, "I . . . I'm sorry, Matt. I didn't know."

"Sure you didn't. And while you're thinking about how cruel I am, just remember that I could have laid you before I laughed. Now beat it."

I unlocked the door and opened it for her, and locked it again behind her, and listened to her footsteps receding down the hall outside until they were no longer audible. Then I drew a long breath, wondering if I'd just perpetrated a tactical mistake or a stroke of genius.

On the one hand, Monk might wonder how I'd spotted his girl so quickly, but she'd betrayed herself in lots of ways and it had been a pretty obvious plant anyway, so obvious that it would have looked more suspicious if I'd played along with it. That's what a clever man who was interested in getting something on the Monk would have done. I was trying to establish that I didn't give a damn about Monk and his people as long as they left me alone.

I was a little ashamed of the sob story I'd used on the girl. It was quite true, of course. That was why I was ashamed of it. It's never nice to have to play games with your own emotions. But there's no excuse for making enemies unnecessarily. Whether or not Jill was the contact I was looking for, she seemed to be a young agent with a reasonable amount of brains and guts, and I didn't want her hating me. It might just possibly make a difference later, when the chips were down.

I'd had to reject her pretty roughly to make it look good—and sound good for any mikes that might have been planted in the room—and there's only one excuse a woman will accept for such a deadly insult: that it was done by a man with a broken heart. I decided that I'd been pretty smart, after all, and that I should be pretty proud of myself. I should feel real good about my diabolical cleverness: Helm the human calculating machine, unaffected by sex or sentiment. The bad taste in my mouth was undoubtedly caused only by too much rum.

While I was telling myself this, the telephone rang. I went over and picked it up. The voice at the other end was feminine, but it wasn't Jill Darnley's voice. I couldn't place it at once.

"Mr. Helm?"

"This is Helm," I said.

"This . . . this is Isobel McLain." The voice sounded oddly slurred and uncertain. "Room sixteen-dash-two. That's on the ground floor of cottage sixteen, over by the paddle-tennis court. Would you . . . would you come at once? The door will be unlocked; just walk in. Please hurry."

I started to speak, perhaps to ask a silly question, but the connection had already been broken at the other end.

Chapter Six

I CHECKED THE loads in the snub-nosed, five-shot .38 caliber revolver I'd been issued in Washington, and I checked the spare cartridges in their tricky little quick-feed case. Being designed for police use, it holds six rounds: most cop guns shoot six times. I've never felt the need for that much firepower, but then I'm not a cop.

I took my knife from my pocket and made certain it would open smoothly if needed. It looks like an ordinary jackknife, just a little larger than average, but it has some special features. For instance, the long blade locks into place when opened so it won't fold over and cut off your fingers if you happen to hit bone as you go in. I made sure I had my new belt on—it has some special features, too—and I got the little drug kit we often carry and slipped that into a concealed pocket.

I guess this seems like a lot of preparation, but I tend to be a trifle suspicious of breathless midnight telephone invitations from mysterious ladies in distress.

Turning to leave, I stopped, looking at the orchid lei Jill had been wearing, still lying on the chair where she'd dropped it. I picked it up, wondering how to get it back to her, but decided that the conscientious gesture would be out of character for the surly, brooding bastard I was supposed to be—besides, the damn island was lousy with orchids. She wouldn't have any trouble finding more if she wanted them. I made a face at the pretty necklace of flowers, dropped it into the wastebasket, turned out the lights, and left the room.

Just down the hall was an outside staircase leading to the ground. I took this, with my hand in my coat pocket and my gun in my hand. Once I was covered by the garden shadows below, I took the hand and the gun out of my pocket.

It was a fine place for dirty work at night. There was

an occasional light but it didn't reach very far through the lush foliage. The path was a tunnel through giant ferns and overhanging palms, not to mention such exotics as bird-of-paradise trees, the flowers of which actually do look like brilliant birds. Not that I could identify them in the dark, or would have taken the time if I could, but I'd kind of checked them out that morning, returning from the beach. I'd also located the paddle-tennis layout, where a kind of bastard court game could be played with what looked like overgrown Ping-pong paddles. You never know when a little local geography is going to come in handy.

There was nobody on the court when I reached it. The deserted spectator tables sprouted beach umbrellas that looked like giant mushrooms in the dark. There were no lights in the adjacent building, but a lamp on a post let me read the number on the nearest door: 16-2. As I moved that way, my foot nudged something on the walk that skidded away with a rattling, fragile little sound. I found the object and picked it up: a pair of glamorized sunglasses that looked familiar. They were unbroken. Remembering the shaky voice on the phone, I wondered if the owner could say the same.

The door was the usual flimsy fresh-air affair with ventilating slats instead of solid panels. It opened silently when I turned the knob, and let me into a shadowy porch or lanai, similar to the one in my own suite. The walls were striped with the light filtering through the louvered doors and window shutters. Beyond, presumably, was the bedroom. It was quite dark in there.

I'd already stuck my neck out coming this far; I might as well stick it out all the way. If I'd really wanted to avoid a trap, I'd have stayed in my room. You can learn a lot about people from the kind of traps they set, if you live through the experience. I stepped into the darkness and stumbled over something soft on the floor. A light came on.

"Welcome, Mr. Helm," said Isobel McLain's voice. "Thank you for responding so promptly to my call."

I wheeled to face her. She was sitting in one of the large beds jutting out from the left-hand wall, and she was unarmed and more or less undressed; that is, she was wearing nothing but an insubstantial nightgown of the pale café-au-lait color that makes a woman's skin look very white by contrast. She had nice shoulders, I noticed. This was the glamorous part of the display.

The unglamorous part was that she was holding a small hotel towel to the side of her head. There was fresh blood on the towel and on her hand. Her hair was matted on that side. Her face was shiny and drawn with pain.

"No, Mr. Helm," she said tartly, as if I had spoken. "I did not fall down drunk and bump my head. Look at my room!"

I looked at her room. It had been pretty well torn apart. Dresser drawers and closed doors gaped open, and feminine stuff was all over the place. At my feet, in a crumpled heap, was the black dress she'd worn at the cocktail party. This was what I'd stumbled on in the dark. It seemed to have picked up some dust and blood since I'd last seen it. Her purse lay beside it. Farther on in the direction of the bathroom lay her discarded underwear, shoes, and stockings.

I couldn't help thinking that women were having a lot of trouble staying in their clothes in Honolulu tonight, judging by one man's experience. Well, this was a good climate for it—not staying in your clothes, I mean. The risk of pneumonia was negligible.

I turned back to the bed and Isobel McLain, and held up the sunglasses I'd found. "You dropped these outside. They seem to be okay." I laid them on a table nearby. "What happened here, Mrs. McLain?"

"There were two men," she said. "One must have been waiting out there in the bushes, watching for me. He must have hit me as I approached the door, while I was busy rummaging in my purse for my key. I say 'must have' because I don't really know what happened. Suddenly I was down on hands and knees and my head was full of pain and there was something wet running down my neck. Foolishly enough, all I could think of was that I was wrecking my nylons on the concrete walk—I could feel them going—and that I must look very ridiculous and undignified. Is that a normal reaction, Mr. Helm?"

I shrugged. "It's been a long time since I wore a pair of nylons, ma'am. Or worried about my dignity."

She laughed softly, and winced. "Don't be funny. It hurts my head. Well, after a moment or two I sort of felt the man standing over me, and I was terrified that he'd hit me again, so I pretended to collapse into total unconsciousness. He dragged me in here, and I heard him telling the other man to finish up in a hurry and never mind putting anything back. After a little, the other man said it was no use, the bitch was too smart, there was nothing here to connect her with Helm, even though she'd been seen to make contact with him at the party, earlier. That's what he said, that we'd made contact. Did we make contact, Mr. Helm?"

"I wasn't aware of it," I said. "Not in an official sense of the word. But I guess it could have looked like a contact to somebody watching."

She said, "One day you'll have to explain to me all about contacts, when I don't have such a headache. Anyway, the two men left. When I was sure they weren't coming back, I struggled out of my clothes and into a pretty nightie and called you." She managed a smile. "After all, one can't entertain a gentleman in a dirty dress and laddered stockings, can one?"

I grinned. "Maybe not, but one seems to be able to think pretty fast, even with a bad crack on the head. Why me? Why not the police?"

"What could the police do except make trouble for everybody, including me? I came to Honolulu to rest, Mr. Helm, and to enjoy myself a little if possible, not to answer a policeman's silly, suspicious questions. It's not as if I'd been robbed. I've lost nothing that the police can get back for me, have I? But there is a certain amount of damage. I called you because your name was mentioned. I thought it might be worth something to you not to have me tell this to the authorities."

I regarded her for a moment. It was the first time I'd seen her without the sunglasses. Her eyes were gray. They had a glint of humor in them. She didn't look like the type to say what she'd just said, even with a bloody towel against her head.

I said in a tentative way, "Blackmail, Mrs. McLain?"

Her smile was a little stronger this time. "Of course, Mr. Helm. What did you expect?"

"What do you want?"

She laughed her soft laugh. "Why, my dear man. I want you to clean up this mess, since you seem to be, indirectly at least, responsible for it. I want you to take a look at this bump on my head and tell me if I need a doctor. And if I do, I want you to get me one who'll keep his mouth shut."

"Why?"

"I didn't come clear to Hawaii to have my name plastered all over the newspapers. My loving husband would laugh himself sick. He'd say that's what I got for going off alone."

It wasn't the strongest argument in the world, but I didn't challenge it. Instead I said, "What makes you think I can find you a silent-type doctor?"

She glanced at the gun I still held. "Don't be silly. A man who carries one of those things usually knows his way around, doesn't he?"

"And that's all you want?" I put the revolver away.

She smiled again. "I'm afraid you've been associating with the wrong kind of people. Did you think I was going to hold you up for money?"

"It's been tried. For money, and for other valuable considerations."

"And I'm sure you gave the extortioner a very rough time in every instance. You look like a man who would. But I feel that my demands are quite reasonable, don't you? I mean, it does seem to be because of you that I was honored by this visit, or should I say visitation?" She frowned. "I'm going to try not to pry into your business, at least not yet. I have a certain amount of discretion, and it warns me not to question a man carrying a large pistol, presumably loaded. But maybe you'll condescend to tell me: does every lady you encounter for a moment at a cocktail party receive this kind of attention? If so, I should think it would soon put a blight on your social life."

"I'm afraid we just happened to meet at the wrong moment," I said. "Apparently it caused the wrong people to jump to the wrong conclusions."

"I see." She hesitated. "Do you know an individual named Rath, Mr. Helm? Lawrence Rath?"

"Not under that name," I said. "Why?"

"I said there were two men involved. Now I think of it, I believe there were three. There was also a man who'd just struck up an acquaintance with me in the cocktail lounge or whatever you call it—that pavilion place—and insisted on buying me drinks. At the time, of course, I thought he was just plying me with liquor for the usual reasons; that's why I walked out on him. I decided he was too obvious to be entertaining. Now I wonder if he wasn't just trying to keep me from my room long enough for the other two to finish searching it." She glanced at me sharply. "You don't know him? A rather intriguing-looking man, with the shoulders of an ape and the face of a fallen angel."

Well, it was about time the Monk showed his face locally, as well as his voice. I grinned at Isobel McLain. "That's great poetry, ma'am," I said, "but it doesn't constitute much of a description. I'm afraid my acquaintance doesn't boast many angels, fallen or otherwise. Apes, now that's a different matter."

She was watching me shrewdly. "You use a lot of words, Mr. Helm, but none of them say no. I think you do know the man I mean." After a moment she shrugged. "Well, all right. Just fix up this place so I can sleep in it and the maid won't have hysterics in the morning."

I moved toward the bed. "If you don't mind, I'd like to see about that bump on your head first. Did you get a look at either of the two men in here?"

"You over-estimate my courage. I kept my eyes tightly closed and acted just as dead as I could. . . . Ouch!"

"Sorry," I said, leaning over to part the hair above her ear. Whether or not she was genuine—a question I hadn't answered to my own satisfaction—her blood certainly was. "Well, you have a small scalp nick, about a quarter of an inch long," I reported after a brief examination.

"Is that all? From the way it's been bleeding, I thought I'd been slashed to the bone."

"Head wounds often bleed a lot," I said. "I don't think you need a doctor for that. It's too small to require stitching. However, there's no telling what's under it. I mean, you could have a concussion, or even a fracture."

"Wouldn't I have been knocked out completely, if it were that serious?"

"Not necessarily."

"If it were yours, would you see a doctor about it?"

I said, "That's beside the point. Let's say that I know from experience that my skull is fairly durable."

She said, "Well, suppose I just take it easy for a day or so. Then if my eyes begin to cross or I have dizzy spells or start stuttering or something, we can consult the medical profession. In the meantime, why don't you bring in a wet washcloth and help me get rid of this gore? I washed off some of it, but I felt too awful, standing up, to get it all. And make me a drink. There's Scotch over there on the dresser."

"No drinks," I said. "Not with a possible concussion."

She looked up irritably. "Mr. Helm, if I'd wanted real medical advice, I'd have called a real doctor. Now make me a drink like a good boy, and if it scrambles my brains I'll remember that you advised against it. Is that satisfactory?"

"Yes, ma'am," I said humbly.

"And bring my sleeping pills here so I'll have them handy. They're in the medicine thing in the bathroom."

"Sure," I said. "Your life's your own, Mrs. McLain. If you insist on ending it tonight, who am I to stand in your way?"

"What do you mean?" she demanded.

"People have died from mixing alcohol and barbiturates. Add to the mixture a nasty bump on the noggin, and the results should be very interesting. Where did you say you kept those pills?"

She sighed. "My God, you're just a little mine of information, aren't you? All right, I'll settle for the Scotch. No ice. A dash of water. Tell me, Mr. Helm, with that gun you must be one of three things: a criminal, a policeman, or a secret agent. Which is it?"

"Can't I be just a man with a gun?" I asked. "No? All right, then, I'm an agent."

"You said that a little too easily. An agent of what, or should I say, of whom?"

"Of the U. S. Government, naturally. Would I say Russia or China even if it were true?"

"If you're telling the truth—I don't say I believe you, but if you are—does that make those other men Russian or Chinese?"

"Those are certainly two possibilities," I said, and hesitated, but it didn't seem like the time or the place for long-winded explanations, true or false. I had a hunch she was a lady who'd be intrigued by mystification, so I took refuge in security. "I'm afraid that's as much as I can tell you, Mrs. McLain."

"I see." She shrugged her pretty shoulders. "Well, I must say you're damn slow with the drinks. . . . Ah, thanks." She took the glass I offered her. By the time I returned with a wrung-out washcloth, it was half empty. I cleaned the blood off her fingers and got what she'd missed on her face and neck. She kept her eyes closed during most of this operation, but suddenly she opened them and looked up with a hint of malice. "How do you feel, Mr. Helm?"

I didn't pretend not to catch her meaning. "Frustrated," I said. "Being a gentleman, I obviously can't make a pass at a lady with concussion of the brain. But you could have picked a more discreet nightie, ma'am."

She laughed. "That was nicely said. I was feeling very

unattractive, but you reassure me. Now try to tidy up the room a bit. You've been married, haven't you?"

"Yes," I said.

"It shows on a man. Well, then, you shouldn't have too much trouble putting my belongings back in some kind of order; you'll know how a woman likes her things. And tomorrow you'll take me to lunch and tell me all about yourself and your mysterious work. At the Royal Hawaiian, I think. Yes, the Royal Hawaiian, with all those bright, brittle people showing off for each other. I don't expect you to compromise your silly security, of course. All you have to do is answer my impertinent questions with amusing lies. And then we'll settle on a nice place to have dinner together. . . . Yes, Mr. Helm?"

I said, "Skip it. You're old enough to know your own mind."

She smiled slowly. "You know, that's quite true if not very flattering. And I'm also old enough to understand that continuing to associate with you may involve me in more disagreeable situations like this one. That's what you were going to point out to me, wasn't it?"

"Yes."

She said, "Mr. Helm, I'm fully aware of it, and I think it's wonderful. I've been bored to tears ever since I came to Honolulu. If there's anything duller than a bunch of people cavorting about in skimpy bathing suits, it's a bunch of people cavorting about in silly native costumes. Most fashionable resorts display only one of these aberrations; here you get both. I tell you, I've been bored practically to suicide for the best part of a week, but it's a funny thing, Mr. Helm: tonight I have a splitting headache, my room looks like a junk yard, I've ruined a pair of perfectly good nylons and got blood all over an expensive dress—but I'm not bored any longer. So tomorrow I want you to take me to lunch, and I want you to be sure to bring your gun. I've never had lunch with a man wearing a gun. Now make me another drink, like a good boy, and clean up this rat's nest, and get out of here so I can go to sleep."

"Yes, ma'am."

As I got to work, I was aware of her watching me in a speculative way, like a farmer who's bought a horse and wonders if he's made a good deal. Whatever she was, I decided, she was pretty good. If she was, as she'd intimated, just a hard-drinking society woman looking for screwball kicks, she at least had a certain amount of courage, to take the night's events in her stride and risk more of the same.

And if, as seemed quite possible, she was something else entirely, it was still a good act well performed. In either case, it looked as if I wasn't going to be suffering from loneliness if she had her way.

Well, I hadn't been feeling exactly neglected in Honolulu even before she came along.

Chapter Seven

IN THE MORNING I went swimming again, on the theory that it's not a bad idea, in critical times, to give the impression of being a creature of habit. It has been known to throw people off guard, even people who should know better. Besides, I was kind of curious to see if Jill would show up for our surfing date after what had happened between us last night. I wasn't laying any bets either way, since the decision wasn't hers, but the Monk's, and I couldn't predict how clever he'd try to be.

It was another clear tropical morning, with the sky brightening behind the rim of volcanic rock to the east of Waikiki, but today I didn't have the sunrise to myself. Down the beach a little way, a couple of pretty, sleepy-looking girls in bikinis were being entertained by a couple of husky, wide-awake young men wearing sawed-off khaki trunks and military dog tags. I assumed they were off the transport we'd seen heading into port the night before, and I admired the speed with which they had established diplomatic relations with the natives.

They barely noticed me as I braved the cool morning

waves very briefly. Afterward, I took a long time drying myself and sat on the sea wall for a while just looking at the ocean. I was a little surprised, as I had been before, at the lack of traffic out there. It was my impression that in good weather just about anywhere along the edge of the American continent in summer you'd see multitudes of assorted vessels day and night. Here, off the largest harbor in the Islands, one distant freighter was the only ship in sight.

There were no pleasure craft visible at all, except for a couple of the twin-hulled, sloop-rigged catamarans used for taking tourists for nautical joy-rides. They were being made ready down the beach for the day's business. I wondered idly about the deserted ocean: maybe these waters were too dangerous for small boats, for reasons hidden from a landlubber like me. . . .

"Oh, there you are!" said Jill's voice. "When I didn't see you, I thought . . . I was afraid you'd decided not to come."

I looked up. She was wearing a different bathing suit this morning—if you could call it a suit—and the guy who'd invented checked blue gingham would have wept to see what she was doing to a couple of scraps of his theoretically demure and modest material. She had the same old red board on her head, however.

I said, "Hell, are you still around, Sexy? I figured after last night's flop, you'd run to Big Brother and have him find you somebody easier to seduce."

Jill turned pink. "I . . . I brought another board," she said resolutely after a moment.

"My God, you're a real little optimist." I said. "If I don't trust you on dry land, what makes you think I'm going to trust you in forty feet of water?"

"It's not that deep," she said. "Just a minute. Let me get rid of this one." She started toward the water's edge, and looked back awkwardly, hampered by her unwieldy burden. "Please? Be nice, Matt. You know I'm only obeying orders."

"That's what the commandant of Auschwitz said as he fired up his ovens each morning." I sighed and rose.

"Oh, all right. Where is this damn board? I suppose you've got it rigged so it'll either blow me up or sink me. . . ."

The boys with the dog tags revised their opinions of me steeply upward when they saw what I'd drawn for a surfing instructor. They stared so hard and so long that their girls turned audibly peevish. Meanwhile I was learning how to stand on a surfboard in shallow water, not the easiest balancing act in the world, even with Jill to steady the thing. After I'd fallen off three times, she said I had the general idea, and got her own board, and demonstrated the prone paddling technique. You could also paddle kneeling, she said, but I'd better not try that until I got my equilibrium working a little better.

It was quite a lesson. Just getting out there wasn't easy and catching a wave right, even with Jill to give me the timing and an initial shove, seemed for a while to be next to impossible. I hadn't tackled a new sport for a good many years, and I'd forgotten how clumsy a reasonably well-coordinated man can be when he really tries.

Then a big one came along, curling nicely as it reached us, and she pushed me off and called to me to stand up, as she had half a dozen times before. This time, however, I made it all the way to my feet without falling off, and as I found my balance I felt the thing really start to go. It was a strange sensation, hissing shoreward on a tender, tricky little plank with the wave roaring angrily right astern. I saw how it could become habit-forming, like skiing or auto racing.

I rode it clear out, and dropped down at last, and paddled back out to where Jill sat on her board, waiting for me.

"Not too bad," she said. "Now on the next one, try to steer it a little, just to get the feel. Throw your weight back a bit and tilt the board in the direction you want to go. You're not going to be able to ride big surf straight off like this, you know. You'll want to turn at once, the minute you catch the wave, and slide across the face of it, away from the break. . . . Matt?"

"Yes?"

"Who's the frigid brunette, anyway? The one you were talking to at the party?"

I grinned. "What makes you think she's frigid?"

"Sorry. Didn't mean to insult your dreamboat. I hope you had a lovely time in her room last night."

I said, "You're just jealous because I spurned you for another woman. Maybe I'm tired of tanned blondes. I could also get tired of being watched all the time."

"That would be tough," she said coolly. "Real tough. Take it up with Washington, Matt. You know there's nothing I can do about it. And you haven't answered my question."

I said, "If she's anything but Mrs. Kenneth McLain from Washington, D.C., I don't know about it."

Jill said, "She may be Mrs. Kenneth McLain, but she's not from Washington, D.C. We've checked her out that far already. And she was asking for you here. Before you arrived. Here at the hotel."

I thought this over for a moment. "Thanks for the tip," I said. "I had a hunch she was a little too good to be true. So that's why Monk decided to have her room searched. I wondered. Of course you could be lying to me."

"Of course," Jill said, smiling.

I grimaced. "Well, whatever she is, tell your friends that batting folks over the head with gun barrels is clumsy technique, not to mention the fact that it's hard on the guns. There are plenty of other ways to take people out of action."

"How did you know it was a gun barrel?"

"A sap wouldn't have cut the scalp that way. You're sure she was inquiring about me? Before I came?"

"Quite sure." Jill glanced past me. "Outside! Get ready. See if you can catch this one all by yourself. When I say go, paddle like hell. . . . Go!"

I felt the lift of the wave, stroked hard with both arms, and felt the board start to plane; then the nose dug into solid water, the rear end rose, and I was thrown off. Half the Pacific Ocean landed on top of me. I clawed myself to the surface, retrieved the board, and returned to Jill. She wasn't laughing when I got there, but that wasn't saying she hadn't laughed earlier.

"That's known as pearling, or pearl diving," she said. "You had your weight too far forward, so your board just dove for the bottom. Are you tired? You've been at it for almost an hour."

I said, "Let's see if I can't make just one more reasonably good ride so I know I've got the idea." I kicked my feet a bit to keep my board from swinging away from hers, and looked down into the clear water, some six feet deep. The coral down there looked brown and slimy alive, not bright and clean like the dead stuff you see in the stores. I said, "I hope you don't have any sharks around here. California's having a rash of them, from what I read in the papers."

Jill shrugged. "Oh, once in a while somebody reports seeing one, generally a hysterical tourist."

"Yeah," I said dryly, "I know those hysterical tourists with arms and legs bitten off. You can't trust those people not to exaggerate."

Jill laughed, and we waited for a wave, rocking gently so far from the beach that it felt like the middle of the ocean. I'd never been so far offshore without a real boat to support me, but I was gaining confidence in my board and my swimming ability—it occurred to me that I'd been doing a lot of swimming lately, in various parts of the world, with various companions, some of whom were no longer alive. It wasn't a happy train of thought, and I shunted it out of my mind.

The sun was up now and the water was suddenly warm and pleasant. The beaches were filling with bathers. A couple of tiny sailboats had ventured out from shore and were jockeying around to seaward of us. Both of them caught a wave at an outer line of breakers and came planing in toward us. One got crosswise and capsized, but the two kids in bathing suits flipped it back up with hardly an effort and scrambled back aboard, laughing.

I swung my board around, expecting the same wave to reach us, but it died before it got that far and rolled by as a smooth and useless swell. I watched a water-skier go by far out, bouncing along behind a small speedboat with an enormous outboard motor. It seemed kind of unnecessary to get hauled around the ocean by all that horsepower when there were waves you could slide on for free.

"Matt?" Jill said.

"Yes," I said.

"Is that what you really think?"

"What?"

"What you're reported to have said in Washington. About . . . about our involvement in Asia."

I regarded her for a moment, with some irritation. She was straddling her red board casually, riding it like a horse, obviously just as comfortable on it as a cowboy in his favorite saddle. Her soaked blonde hair streamed down her back, and her slender body, practically naked, was brown and wet and intriguing. I was annoyed with her for breaking the pleasant, lazy mood of the morning. I was even tempted to play along with her a little, just to maintain our happy relationship, but it would have been out of character and I couldn't take the chance.

I said, "Too bad, kid. We could have had a lot of fun together in the line of duty. Maybe some day you'll learn not to press too hard. See you on shore."

I flopped down on my board and headed for the hotel. I heard her calling my name, but I kept on paddling. Pretty soon I heard the splash of her strokes behind me and the hiss of her board going through the water much faster than mine—she really knew how to drive the thing.

"Matt!" she said, drawing alongside. "Matt, wait! I didn't mean—"

I stopped paddling. We coasted along side by side, losing speed. "I suppose you've got a waterproof tape recorder buried somewhere in this balsa," I said grimly.

"It isn't balsa, it's polyurethane," she said. "And there's no recorder."

"Well, it'll sound good in the report, anyway. 'By shrewd interrogation, subject was led to confirm political

opinions attributed to him, saying, quote . . .' " I shook
my head. "Baby, do you really think I'm stupid enough
to pull the same boner twice? Okay, so I once made a
casual statement in answer to what I thought was a
casual question, which was my mistake. Maybe I was
even drunk enough to try to back up my opinion when
it was challenged, but I'm sober now, and I'm clear out
of the casual-statement business. Anybody who wants to
know what I think about anything political is going to
have to use scopolamine or pentothal in large doses.
Do I make myself clear?"

"Matt, I—"

"As for you, doll," I went on without letting her speak,
"I know you've got orders to keep an eye on me, and to
worm your way into my confidence, if possible. I wasn't
holding it against you. Hell, I even gave you a break
last night; I could have let you make a complete fool of
yourself, instead of just half a fool. So what do I get for
thanks? A damn little agent-provocateur trying to con
me into making incriminating statements, by God!"

She licked her lips. "You're wrong! I asked because
. . . because I really want to know. Because I believe
exactly as you're supposed to believe!"

"Well now, isn't that sweet!" I looked at her coldly.
"So we're just political soulmates, are we? Honey, that
gag is almost as old as the please-help-me-off-with-my-
dress routine you tried yesterday. You'd better tell Monk
to get a new writer on the job. This script stinks." I dug
at the water with both hands. "So long, Jill. Thanks for
the lesson. As an agent you make a great surfing teacher."

"Matt, wait!" she called. "There's something I have to
tell you. It's about . . . about birds. Seabirds, Matt!"

Well, it was about time she made up her mind.

Chapter Eight

I SWUNG MY board around, not as easy a job as it sounds, since it had a kind of skeg or tail fin to make it run straight. But I got it turned and paddled back to where she was sitting on hers, eyeing me resentfully.

"Damn you!" she said. "I didn't want—"

"Never mind your didn't-wants," I said. "Turn your head a bit when you talk. There's probably somebody keeping an eye on us from shore. If he's just using binoculars, we're okay, but if he's got a good big telescope he might be able to read lips, even at this distance. You're sure the boards are clean? You checked them this morning?"

"Yes, of course, I checked them! I knew I might have to tell you—"

"Well, tell me," I said.

"There are few seabirds on the Islands," she said stiffly.

"Yes, but the landbirds are very numerous," I said.

She drew a long breath. "Damn you, I didn't want to have to talk to you yet. The more talk, the bigger the risk. Why did you have to act so impossible, both last night and this morning? You knew somebody would be contacting you sooner or later. You might have known I could be the one—as a matter of fact, I grabbed at this assignment so I'd be able to communicate with you quickly when the right time came. And then you went out of your way to make things absolutely impossible for me! Why?"

"Among other things, to make up your wishy-washy little mind for you, if you were the one," I said rudely. "And to get rid of you if you weren't."

Jill said angrily, "Well, I don't like the way you're acting! My agreement with Washington—"

"Keep your face away from shore," I said. "Who the hell are you to make agreements at the expense of the rest of us, Jill? Anyway, you made your deal with Washington. You didn't make it with me. And you've already cost one man his life, trying to play it so damn safe. I'm not about to be number two if I can help it."

"That's not fair!" she gasped. "It wasn't my fault that Naguki—"

"Naguki was playing lightning rod to your barn, baby. Under orders. He took the discharge meant for you. Well, I don't conduct electricity and I have no desire to learn how. And I gave you the bird-cue last night. Since you didn't speak up then and let me know who you were, you're hardly in a position to complain because I haven't behaved properly toward you." I shook my head quickly as she started to protest. "That's enough of that; we can't sit here arguing all day. Give it to me quick. What have you got so far? What's the Monk up to?"

"I . . . I don't know yet."

I said sourly, "That's a big help. What *do* you know, yet?"

"Don't talk to me like that!" she snapped. "What right have you got to criticize? You haven't lived with this for weeks, like I have, expecting every minute to be found out and. . ." She shivered. "You don't know what Monk is like, what he can do."

It was no time to start an argument about who knew more about the Monk than whom. I said, "I left my crying-towel on the beach, honey, or I'd be more than happy to lend it to you. But suppose you just get real brave and wipe your nose on your finger and let me know just what you *have* got for me. If anything."

"Why, you overbearing, insufferable . . . !" She stopped. I grinned at her. After a moment, she laughed reluctantly, which was a relief. I'd been starting to wonder whether I'd misjudged her completely when I'd decided she possessed enough nerve and intelligence to be worth cultivating. Tackling the Monk and the organization he'd built out here with nothing but a gutless ingenue for support wasn't really an enticing prospect. But she did laugh; there was hope for her yet. "All right," she breathed. "All right, I get the message, Matt.

But you can't blame me for being scared. It's the first time I've done anything like this."

I said, "Don't get your hopes up. You'll be just as scared the second time, and the twenty-second. After a while you'll simply discover that people don't really die of fright."

She made a face at me. "That's very encouraging! Thanks a lot! What do you want to know?"

"Start with the political bit. Where does that fit in?"

"What do you mean?"

"What's the connection between the political opinions you seem to hold and your signing up with us—that is, with Monk. And how did you get from there to letting Washington know all about it? I mean, are you seriously opposed to what's going on in Asia, as you suggested a few minutes ago?"

"Of course I'm seriously opposed, aren't you?" she said sharply. "That's exactly why I joined. Monk promised us there'd be a chance to help. To put a stop to all the terrible things we're doing to those poor people over in—"

I sighed. "Stay off the soapbox, honey, please. Don't try to tug at my old heartstrings. Who's us?"

"Why, all the latest recruits. Matt—"

"How many?"

"I don't know. Half a dozen, I suppose, but you know how it is, we're kept from knowing each other as much as possible. I've only met a few of the others, the ones I recommended myself. Monk asked me to suggest a few names. Matt—"

"They're all young people like you? With the same mushy ideas?"

"Yes, of course. I mean—" She glared at me. "Matt, are you trying to tell me that you don't really believe what you're supposed to've said in Washington?"

I said, "What I said was based on strategy, not sentiment, honey. If you want to know the truth, atrocities bore hell out of me."

"Then . . . then I feel sorry for you! You've been in this horrible business so long you're no longer human!"

"That," I said dryly, "is a distinct possibility, but I fail to see how it's relevant to the subject at hand, any more than my political beliefs. I'm not here to do research for a polemic article. I'm here to do a job, and you're supposed to feed me the information I need to do it. So far I feel damn undernourished, information-wise." I scowled at her. "Let's get it straight now. Do I gather that Monk is also opposed to our military posture in Asia, to use the jargon? And that he recruited you and some other idealistic kids by promising you a crack at leading the world back to peace and happiness?"

"Yes," she said sulkily. "Yes, he was . . . very persuasive."

"He can be," I agreed. "When his ascetic face lights up with burning enthusiasm and he gets that fanatic look in his bright blue eyes. . . . It's one of his biggest assets. You should have seen him playing a dedicated Heil-Hitler boy some years back; he was damn convincing. What woke you up, Jill? What broke the hypnotic spell?"

"Nothing broke the spell," she said stiffly. "There wasn't any spell. I wasn't hypnotized. I'm not a child, Matt; I knew what I was doing. And I haven't changed my opinions in the least!" She hesitated. "I . . . I just didn't realize how far he intended to go. In spite of what people seem to think, the fact that you're opposed to your country's foreign policy doesn't necessarily mean . . . Well, I don't like what's being done in Washington, but that doesn't mean I prefer Moscow or Peking, in this case Peking. And when I learned beyond any doubt that Monk was negotiating with them, and that they were sending a couple of specialists to help. . . ."

"Specialists in what? To help with what?"

She shook her head. "I don't know, Matt. I just haven't been able to find out."

I was beginning to have an uneasy feeling she wasn't ever going to find out anything Monk didn't want her to find out. What worried me even more was the fact that I couldn't help wondering if what she'd already found out was anything the Monk was actually trying to keep hidden. He was too smart and wary to conduct treasonable negotiations in such a way that a green kid could stumble on the evidence, unless he wanted that evidence stumbled on. Which indicated that he must be playing a much trickier game than anybody seemed willing to believe—or maybe I was giving him too much credit. I hoped so.

"Do you know when these specialists are coming?"

"They were supposed to arrive earlier in the week with something Monk needed. I don't have any reason to believe they didn't. Of course I couldn't ask without attracting attention—I wasn't even supposed to know about it—but nobody's been acting as if anything's gone wrong."

"If they did arrive, where would they be now?"

"Well, he wouldn't want them hanging around Oahu, I don't suppose. He'd probably get them to K as soon as possible." She went on quickly, forestalling my question "It's just something I've heard mentioned, Matt, a kind of base or hideout, I gather, where they're getting things ready for what they're going to do. They just refer to it as K. I haven't been able to learn where it is." She paused and went on, "I'm sorry to be so little help. I've been scared to ask questions about it. I can guess, if it's any good."

"Try it and we'll see how good it is."

"K has to be accessible by water, because they go there by boat and sometimes the weather holds them up for days. When the trades are blowing too hard, apparently, they can't make it. Of course they may stop somewhere and switch to a car or a plane but I don't think they do. And if the place is near the water, it probably isn't on an island like this one, with a shore road clear around it. I mean, they wouldn't want fishermen or picnickers stumbling on it by mistake, or seeing the boat coming or leaving. Do you know how the main islands go? There's Kauai, farthest to the northwest, and Oahu, where we are. Then there are Molokai, Maui, and Hawaii, all strung out to the southeast beyond Diamond Head over there." She started to lift her hand.

"Don't point!" I said sharply.

"Sorry," she said, abashed. "Anyway, Oahu itself is out because of roads, I think, and so are Maui and the Big Island, Hawaii. Well, there are some desolate places along the shoreline of Hawaii that might do, but it's a long boat ride, too long to be really feasible, a couple hundred miles. Even if you wanted to risk it in the speedboats they use, they don't have the cruising range, and I've never seen them take extra gas. Also, I've clocked them out and in, when I could do it safely. Sometimes they're gone for several days, of course, but once in a while they're back in six hours or less. You couldn't get to Hawaii and back in that time, not in the fastest boat in the Islands. You'd have to be averaging over sixty knots in open water. The boats they have are lucky to do thirty-five wide open in a sheltered lagoon."

My opinion of her was rising again; at least she'd got some facts and done some thinking about them. "Where do these speedboats hang out?" I asked.

"Right here in the Honolulu yacht basin. There are two of them, registered under different owners—one outboard and one inboard—but only one is there now, the outboard. The other's been missing since two nights ago. They usually make the trip at night. I suppose it's at K. Maybe it took the Chinese delegation over with whatever they brought."

"But you don't know what that is?"

"No."

"Does Monk have some kind of house or headquarters around here?"

"Yes, he's renting a big house in a fashionable district behind Diamond Head, under the name of Rath. It's a pink house with a swimming pool—"

"Never mind that," I said. "I'm not about to play detective around there unless the situation changes drastically. Let's get back to K. Say you're right, and we can eliminate Oahu, Maui, and Hawaii. What about the smaller islands? There are some, aren't there?"

"Well, Lanai is just a big pineapple plantation. It's low and flat and pretty well cultivated. I can't see it as a hideout. Kahoolawe is used by the military for bombing practice. It's in restricted waters and any private boat sticking its nose in there would be challenged at once. Niihau is privately owned and strangers would be very conspicuous. And that's about it. Of course there are plenty of small, deserted islets along the coasts, but most of them are just volcanic rocks sticking out of the water, hard to land on and mostly visible from shore, so any unusual activity would attract attention." She shook her head. "I think it's on one of the main islands close by. There's a stretch on the northwest coast of Kauai that's pretty deserted. I suppose K could be there."

"But you obviously don't think it is," I said. "Let's hear your real theory."

"I think it's on Molokai," she said. "That's only some thirty miles southeast of here, within easy range of a fast boat in good weather, and it has all of the qualifications. I'd be willing to bet five to one on Molokai."

"The leper colony?"

"Please, Mr. Helm! We call it Hansen's disease these days."

"And old fogies are senior citizens, and house trailers are mobile homes," I said grimly. "Three cheers for the age of double-talk. But who'd park a hideout in the middle of a bunch of, er, victims of Hansen's disease, with the flesh peeling off the bones? I mean, it's a great cover, but what if you catch the bug?"

Jill laughed. "It isn't nearly as communicable as the old stories would make you think, Matt. Furthermore, contrary to the popular conception, Molokai is a fairly large and pleasant island inhabited mainly by ordinary, healthy people. The Kalaupapa colony occupies just a small, inaccessible peninsula below the sheer cliffs of the north coast. The rest is pineapple, sugar cane, and mountains. Quite high mountains. Five thousand feet or so. They take up the whole northeast corner of Molokai; actually most of the eastern half. There's a road along the south shore, but it barely turns the end of the island. From there back to Kalaupapa on the north side—the windward side—are twenty-odd miles of empty shore on which nobody lives nowadays: some of the wildest coast you can imagine. Mountains rising right out of the sea. Deep gorges, high waterfalls, impenetrable jungles. And Molokai is the least developed of all the islands. It has no tourist accommodations to amount to anything; you wouldn't have to worry about many sightseers or Sunday geologists poking around. I think Molokai is it. It's got to be."

She'd obviously considered the problem carefully, and she knew her Islands. In the absence of stronger information, I wasn't apt to get any better guesses.

I said, "Okay, we'll accept northeastern Molokai as a working hypothesis. Can you pinpoint it any closer? Is there anything else you want to tell me?" She shook her head to both questions. I said, "Then we'd better break this up. What are you going to say when you get ashore?"

She frowned. "What do you mean?"

I said, "Hell, you've got to give them something to chew on. We'll have to hope they didn't have the equipment to catch what we were saying to each other out here, but they couldn't miss me paddling off and you calling me back. What did you say to bring me back?"

"Why . . . why, I hadn't really thought about it."

I said, "Hell, the answer's obvious. You called to me and said you loved me. You said you were crazy about me. That's what made me turn back."

"*What*?" She looked aghast. "Really, Matt . . . !"

I grinned. "Don't act as if it were unthinkable, doll. You'll hurt my feelings. I came back to tell you I thought the gag was in pretty poor taste, and Monk ought to be able to figure out some better lines for you. Okay?"

She hesitated. "But . . . but it's just ridiculous. After all, I only met you yesterday. I couldn't possibly hope to make you believe that I . . . I mean, Monk would think I'd lost my mind, if I told him I'd tried something as foolish and fakey as that."

"Sure," I said. "That's it. You have lost your mind and your heart. To me. Really. And you tried to make me believe it and I wouldn't. That's what we've been arguing about out here. And when you finally half-convinced me you weren't faking, I called you a kooky kid and told you to run along and play with your marbles. Now grab my arm like you were pleading with me. . . . Grab it!"

She reached out obediently and took my arm, pulling our surfboards closer. "But, Matt, if I claim I'm really in love with you and make them believe it, they won't trust me to keep an eye on you!" she protested.

"Now you're getting the idea. What's the use of your being where you can tell me things if you've got nothing to tell me? And how are you going to learn anything hanging around me? Ask to be taken off this job. Say that you're sorry, but you can't trust yourself near my fascinating person, or words to that effect. Maybe they'll put you on something really useful, something that will lead you to K."

"But Monk will suspect—"

I shook my head. "If you act like a lovesick schoolgirl, he may reprimand you but he won't suspect you. Hell, you'd never admit to being mad about me if you really wanted to be close to me so you could pass me information. I'll try to cook up a further diversion of some kind to keep the heat off you. Meanwhile, you locate K. It's a lot to hope that you can get yourself sent there, but one never knows. If you do your lovesick act well enough, Monk may just banish you there to get you away from my influence. If he does, of course, you go."

"But how can I let you know?"

"Don't even try," I said. "Just go. I'll find you somehow. If I don't, it's up to you. You'll have to stop the Monk all by yourself." I looked at her for a moment, and spoke in a flat voice, "Or are you still holding me to that riskless agreement you made with somebody else? If so, doll, you just sneak aboard the next plane heading toward the Mainland. We'll say you've fulfilled your crummy contract. I'll take it from here alone."

She was silent for a moment. When she looked up, her eyes were steady and grave. "All right," she breathed. "All right, Matt. Don't think I don't see what you're doing to me, but all right! I'll try to get sent to K. And if I get killed doing it, I . . . I'll haunt you!"

"Good girl," I said. "Now paddle like hell, like a woman scorned, and go stumbling up the beach with big salty tears running down your face. Drown the phone when you report, incoherently." I disengaged her hand from my arm, and swung her around, and shoved her away from me roughly, for the benefit of the watchers on shore. "Good luck, Jill," I said.

Chapter Nine

WHEN I REACHED THE beach a few minutes behind her, I saw that the sleepy-eyed girls in bikinis were thinking I must be a terrible fellow to send the poor kid off in tears. The boys with the dog tags, on the other hand, were thinking—and saying rather loudly—that I must be a dope from Dopesville to let a chick like that get away from me.

I saw that Jill had left her board on a rack by the sea wall, and I hauled mine over there. I paused briefly to look down at the gaudy red-and-white board, wondering if I'd ever see the owner again alive. She'd have to come up with some very convincing histrionics to fool the Monk. I hoped she was up to them.

Maybe I should have left her in the happy anonymity she'd desired, taking a minimum of risks and doing a minimum of good. But I couldn't help remembering a girl called Claire, who had made no deals with Washington, but had simply gone out and died when the situation called for it. . . .

A thin, dark, hook-nosed man, who'd been sitting at one of the terrace tables watching the view, got up and moved off casually as I approached. He was wearing dark trousers and one of those short-sleeved white summer dress shirts that, worn with a coat and tie, look very respectable indeed. Without the coat, as he was wearing his, they make the most dignified businessman look like an aging Peter Pan. He had a pair of binoculars hanging around his neck. By the size, they probably weren't as strong as ten-power, more likely seven or eight; I didn't think he could have done much lipreading through them. He wasn't anybody whose dossier I'd seen. Apparently the Monk had some reserves he hadn't let Washington know about.

As I crossed the terrace and passed the cocktail pavilion, shuttered at this hour, I met the hotel hostess who'd been working so hard to get us all acquainted the night before. She was a graceful woman of about thirty, quite good-looking in the brown-skinned, black-haired way of the Islands, although the almond shape of her eyes hinted that her ancestry was probably at least as much Oriental as Polynesian. Well, that's Hawaii.

"Good morning, Mr. Helm," she said. "I see you still like your early-morning swim. I hope you're enjoying your stay with us."

"Very much," I said. "Er, I wonder if you could help me out. I didn't quite catch the name of the lady you introduced me to last night, and I'm having lunch with her today, and, well, it's kind of embarrassing to have to ask. . . ."

"Yes, of course. Do you mean Miss Darnley?" She smiled. "I saw the two of you leaving the party together."

"No, the first one. The older one, in the black dress."

"Ah, Mr. Helm, do be careful," the hostess said playfully. "You'll have us thinking you're quite a ladykiller. That was Mrs. McLain, Mrs. Isobel McLain, from your hometown, Washington, D.C. As a matter of fact, she asked to meet you. She said a mutual acquaintance had told her to look you up when she got to Honolulu."

I grinned. "I know, that's why I didn't want to have to ask her what her name was. You know how these mutual-acquaintance deals go. She assumed I knew all about her, and of course I couldn't say I didn't. McLain, eh? Thank you very much."

"Not at all, Mr. Helm."

I watched her move away. She was wearing a long, straight, blue-flowered garment, slit to the knee. The intermittent display of leg was quite effective. I was getting this muu-muu business sorted out now. There was the shapeless, Yankee Mother-Hubbard style originally imposed on the natives in the name of modesty; and then there was the slim oriental cheongsam style, which was a different proposition entirely. It had not been invented to keep susceptible missionaries from being aroused beyond endurance by the naked charms of uninhibited young native girls. On the contrary, it had been designed to make Chinese women attractive to Chinese men. It worked pretty well on other races, too, I decided, watching the hostess walk gracefully out of sight.

Of course, that was quite beside the point. What really mattered was that Jill had apparently not been lying when she suggested that Isobel McLain had known about me before we met. Now it appeared that the woman had even arranged the meeting, in spite of the cool and remote attitude she'd exhibited at the time.

Going toward my room, I rubbed my head hard with my towel, frowning, but it didn't help my cerebral processes in the least. I still couldn't see how this piece fitted into the puzzle itself. It wasn't really surprising, I reflected, since I didn't yet have a very clear view of the puzzle itself. . . .

I smelled cigarette smoke in the hall outside my room. It was drifting out through the slat door. I decided that anybody who intended to murder me wouldn't set fire to a lot of tobacco to warn me, opened the door, and stopped, looking at the man inside. Then I sighed, stepped in, and closed the door behind me.

"Well, it's about time you made a personal appearance," I said. "I was getting a bit fed up with second-hand reports and mysterious telephone calls."

The Monk rose from the armchair in which he'd been sitting and stubbed out his cigarette in the ashtray. I remembered that he had always smoked like a sooty chimney. Apparently it hadn't killed him yet, which was a pity.

"I don't know how you do it," he said admiringly. "I just don't know how you do it, Eric. There must be something about you invisible to the male eye that just bowls them over, old and young."

I said, "Oh, you mean that crazy kid you sicced on me. Has she been phoning in her woes already?"

Monk shook his head enviously. "I just don't know how you do it," he repeated. "Kick them out of bed, give them some corny song-and-dance about a broken heart, and damned if they don't come crawling back asking you to wipe your feet on them. Do you know you've practically ruined a potentially good agent for me?"

I said, "You've got it backwards, haven't you? I didn't ruin her; that's just what she's griping about." I laughed shortly. "You mean the little screwball actually meant all that love-guff she was handing me out there in the surf? Hell, if I'd known that, I'd have played Romeo to her Juliet just to spite you. I thought she was feeding me a line, and a pretty corny one at that."

"I know. She told me. Well, I should have known better than to use a female on you, particularly a young and impressionable one. She won't bother you again."

"That just leaves the older one," I said. "I guess she'll be harder to impress, but I'll give it a whirl."

He was frowning. "The older . . . oh, you mean the McLain?"

I grinned. "Monk, this is Eric, old pal, old pal. Don't pull that blank-faced act on me. Hell, I know the routine as well as you do. You put a tail on me I'm supposed to spot. Then you have a pretty girl make a play for me. When I see through her, too, I get to feeling real smart; I think I've got you all figured out. I accept agent number three as a genuine lady tourist, particularly when she acts as if she doesn't give a damn about me. And most particularly after your boys work her over a bit on some feeble excuse and give her a nice little careful nick in the scalp that bleeds very convincingly. Obviously no attractive woman would allow herself to be messily wounded just to prove she's got nothing to do with you. Obviously. It's only been done a couple of hundred times that I know about."

Monk shrugged. "Think what you please. As a matter of fact, I know nothing about the woman, but if you want to think she's mine, go right ahead."

"Sure," I said, wondering if he could possibly be telling the truth. "Sure."

Monk said in a different tone, "Well, it's been a long time, Eric. Remember the Hofbaden job?"

"I remember," I said.

We stood there facing each other. He had me at a slight disadvantage: he had shoes on. My beach sandals were useless for offense or defense, and bare toes are very vulnerable. In addition to the shoes, he was wearing the usual Hawaiian costume of light pants and a bright, short-sleeved sport shirt. I couldn't spot any weapons, but there undoubtedly were some.

I'd forgotten how massive his shoulders were, and I'd forgotten just how oddly his rather squat, powerful body went with his long, sensitive face, crisp dark hair, and brilliant blue eyes. There was nothing wrong with him physically, I knew, but he gave an impression of deformity nevertheless. He seemed to have been made of parts intended for several different men.

"You're in good shape, Eric," he said softly. "Got a nice tan."

"Thanks. You don't seem to be falling apart much yourself."

"So you're here to take care of me." He said it very casually.

I let myself look mildly surprised. "Hell, I'm here on leave, you know that. Well, let's be polite and call it leave. Disciplinary leave. Suspension is the official term. And if I'd known you were here, I'd have picked somewhere else to sweat it out. But now I'm here, if I have to take care of you to get a little peace and quiet, I guess I can spare the time. You're starting to bother me, amigo. Lay off."

Monk smiled thinly. "And if I don't?"

I grinned at him cheerfully. "Go to hell. What do you

want me to do, flex my muscles at you? I'm giving you fair warning. If you want to have your creeps follow me around at a discreet distance to comply with the official directives, okay. But keep them out of my hair."

He said, "You talk too much. Here, and in Washington, too, apparently. You didn't use to run off at the mouth, Eric."

"Make up your mind," I said. "Last time we conversed, over the phone, you said I always talked too much. I saw a piece about a guy named Naguki in the papers the next day. Yesterday. Seems he fell off a cliff in his car. Or was pushed. What was that all about?"

He shook his head. "Never mind. Maybe I made a mistake calling you on it. Maybe."

I said, "As for Washington, I made my mistake there, as you know, but it won't happen again. You're not going to get a damn thing on me, Monk, much as you'd love to. So just don't waste time trying."

"I think you're faking," he said. "You always were teacher's pet. He wouldn't really slap down his prize pupil like this, not unless he were trying to fool somebody. It smells phony to me."

"For whom am I faking what?" I asked. "For you? What's the matter, have you got a guilty conscience? This mysterious Naguki business and all?" I studied him thoughtfully. "By God, you have! You really think I might have been sent to check up on you! Why? What have you been doing out here you shouldn't?" I laughed aloud. "Well, that makes us even, amigo. You lay off me, or I will get to work and find out why you're running scared. Now get the hell out of here and let me rinse the salt off the body."

His blue eyes regarded me coldly. "You don't fool me, Eric. You don't fool me at all. You never did."

I grinned. "Friend, I never tried to. I merely told you what I wanted and made you like it. And now I'm telling you again. You know and I know and Washington knows that I'm clean. What difference does it make whether or not I approve of what's going on in Asia or anywhere else? Hell, I've killed men for policies I didn't like before now, and I probably will again. That's the way this business works, and everybody knows it. So I tell you again, don't waste everybody's time trying to pin something on me, because there's nothing to pin and because you don't want to annoy me. Do you, Monk? I get awfully damn peevish when I'm annoyed by people who don't do what I tell them. Remember, Monk?"

He remembered, all right. I'd managed to break through to him at last, although I'd had to talk like a boastful jerk to do it. I saw his eyes narrow and his muscles tense, and I figured the first thing I'd better do was kick off those damn sandals as he came for me. But he was older than he had been the last time. He'd learned some things about control that he hadn't known then.

He just wheeled and marched out of the room, closing the door very gently behind him. But I'd got to him. If there had ever been a chance of his leaving me alone, there was none now. I had him sewed up. Well, in a manner of speaking, like the cowboy who lassoed the bear.

I glanced at my watch. It was still early, and I had nothing to do until lunch, which reminded me of Isobel McLain, who'd been asking questions about me, who'd wanted to meet me, and who'd asked me to be sure to bring my gun along on our date because she'd never had lunch with a man with a gun.

I got the weapon out and looked at it. Normally I don't believe in playing games with firearms. Guns are for shooting people or animals, or targets if you have nothing better to do and need the practice. They should be reserved for those purposes only. Play games with knives, if you like, play them with swords or spears or clubs, but leave the damn firearms strictly to the uses for which they were designed, because if you try to be tricky they'll louse you up every time, and somebody'll wind up dead regardless. It might even be you.

That's the principle as it's drilled into us in training, and it's a good one. On the other hand, the woman had given me a clear warning and I'd have been a fool to ignore it. I therefore got out my little tool kit and, being very careful not to leave marks, pulled the bullets out of five cartridges, poured the powder into the john, and flushed it out of sight. Then I stuck the lead bullets back into the empty brass cartridge cases, and reloaded the snub-nosed revolver, now relatively harmless.

I say relatively, because the cases were still primed, and I didn't know how far the explosion of a primer alone, in a powderless case, would kick a pistol bullet. In a long-barreled weapon I'd have been fairly sure the projectile wouldn't even make it all the way to the muzzle against the friction of the rifling, but with a short-barreled gun like this I wasn't sure.

However, if it were now turned against me somehow, it probably wouldn't kill me. And probably I was doing a lovely lady a terrible injustice, and maybe I'd wind up needing the gun with real loads in it and die because, on suspicion, I'd got too clever and armed myself with a weapon that wouldn't shoot. . . .

After getting showered, shaved, dressed, and break-fasted, I spent the rest of the morning studying maps and thinking hard and telling myself firmly I wasn't really responsible for the safety of a girl called Jill, who looked just a little like a girl called Claire, whose safety I hadn't been responsible for either.

Chapter Ten

ISOBEL McLain was late. At least I hoped she was only late, when I knocked on her door and got no response. Whoever she really was, I had a hunch she might prove useful, properly handled. Maybe I shouldn't have voiced my suspicions so openly to Monk, but pretended to play along with the gag, if it was a gag. Maybe he'd decided, since I was wise, to pull Isobel off the job as well as Jill.

And if it wasn't a gag—or at least not the Monk's

gag—there could be more drastic and disturbing reasons for Mrs. McLain's absence. I was just starting to run them through my mind when I heard quick footsteps approaching through the garden, and there she was, dark glasses and all, in a white suit that managed to look summery and smart at the same time, unlike some of this thin summer stuff they wear that's really pretty amorphous.

"I'm terribly sorry," she said, coming up a little breathlessly, which was flattering. I had the impression she was a lady who didn't hurry for just anybody. She even offered an excuse for her tardiness, "I simply had to have my hair done after last night, and the girl took practically forever." She hesitated. "If you want me dressed up, you're going to have to wait a little longer while I change."

I said, "I don't mind waiting, but you look pretty dressed up to me. Judging by what I've seen around here so far, at least half the lady patrons will be dazzling in bedroom slippers and old flour bags."

"Well, all right," she said, smiling. "I guess there's nothing I need in my room." She took my arm as we turned away and leaned close to ask softly, "Did you bring it, as I asked, Mr. Helm?"

"What?"

"The gun."

"Sure." I opened my coat surreptitiously to give her a glimpse of the butt protruding above the waistband of my pants on the left side.

"Is is loaded?"

"Naturally," I said. Well, it wasn't really a lie, the weapon did hold cartridges of a sort. Buttoning my coat again, I went on, "Who'd carry an unloaded gun? Might as well pack around a chunk of scrap iron."

"Do you carry it all the time?"

"It depends. In foreign countries, a gun can cause you more trouble than it's worth. As a matter of fact, firearms are highly overrated implements, particularly short-range firearms like this. There are lots of quieter and tidier ways of killing people close up if you really have to. However, we're on American soil, and I'm not impersonating anybody for whom a gun would be out of character, and as it happens, I may need the damn thing for its moral effect, which is about all it's good for, anyway."

She absorbed this lecture with bright-eyed interest, as if I were recounting a piece of fascinating social gossip. "Don't you use a holster?" she asked. "I thought they were always worn in funny-looking holsters under the left armpit."

I grinned. "That's movie stuff, ma'am. Or gangster stuff. And the F.B.I. likes belt holsters under the coat on the right hip, I understand. They're supposed to do real fancy quick-draw work from that position. But they operate in a more friendly environment, so to speak, than we do. They've got badges to flash if anybody questions the artillery. Me, I'm just as likely to have to get rid of it fast as I am to have to shoot it fast. And getting rid of a gun alone isn't too hard, but just try jettisoning a holster rig that's got your belt through it, or your whole left arm."

"Why, I never thought of that," she said. She laughed happily and tightened her grip on my arm possessively. "And to think that yesterday I was practically bored to extinction with not a ray of excitement in sight!"

"You make it sound real desperate, ma'am," I said. "Was that before you'd checked on my arrival or afterward?" She stopped abruptly, bringing me to a halt as well. I looked up and said, "My God, bananas! Did you know that each banana tree like that produces only one bunch of bananas before it dies clear back to the root? That's kind of sad, when you come to think of it."

She smiled at my irrelevant nonsense. "So you've found me out, Mr. Helm. Well, that's more or less your business, isn't it? Once I learned that you were a professional, I knew I wouldn't fool you very long."

I looked down at her. She was really a very attractive woman, and I liked the calm way she took things. "Are you going to tell me about it, ma'am?"

"Of course," she said. "But suppose you call me Isobel

and I'll call you Matt. Ma'am, indeed! And suppose we claim our table at the Royal Hawaiian before they give it to somebody else. And then suppose we promote me a large double Scotch before we make me lay bare my guilty soul. Sitting under hair dryers always gives me a thirst." She gave me a reproachful glance. "And you haven't even asked how my head is this morning!"

I grinned. "I don't have to ask. I can see there's not a damn thing wrong with your head, inside or out. That's what scares me."

The Monk's moon-faced youth tailed us from the Halekulani in his little Datsun. Well, I hadn't really expected friend Monk to pull everybody off me just because I'd talked tough; I'd have been disappointed if he had. It was a short drive, and soon we were sitting on the terrace of the Royal Hawaiian Hotel, surrounded by important-acting people who seemed to be trying to prove something to each other, I couldn't figure out just what. Isobel picked up her loaded highball when it arrived, saluted me with it, and drank gratefully. She set the glass down and produced a cigarette, which she lit with a butane lighter before I could make like a gentleman. I was glad for the small sign of nervousness. It showed she was human after all.

"All right, first tell me what you already know about me, Matt," she said.

"Well, you're not on any of our lists," I said. "To the best of my recollection, there's nobody who'd meet your description."

"Lists of what?"

"Of local operatives working for nations friendly and unfriendly."

She looked pleased. "Did you really think I might be an agent? A real mystery woman? That's very flattering. I like that. What else do you know?"

"That you probably don't live in the District of Columbia as you claim. That information comes from other people. I haven't checked it personally."

"The other people are quite right. I don't live anywhere near Washington, and McLain isn't my real name. What else?"

"That you nevertheless know the area pretty well."

"I was born practically on the shore of Chesapeake Bay. I went to school in Washington. Go on."

"You've been inquiring about me. You asked the hostess to introduce us." She nodded brightly. I said, "Just one thing before we go on, Isobel. You're having lots of fun, I can see. Well, some people jump out of airplanes for kicks and others play Russian roulette. It's fine with me. I've never believed in making people do things for their own good, or stop doing them. But I feel I ought to point out to you, as I started to last night, that the party can get rough. You've already had a taste of it. I don't know what your game is, but you'd be a lot safer if you played it somewhere else. I've got some unsavory friends and I'm not really a very pleasant guy myself. I mean, if a pretty lady insists on hanging around, I'm apt to start figuring how I can best make use of her—and I don't mean just in bed, although I won't turn that down, either, if it's offered."

There was a little silence. Her face was paler than it had been, and there was anger in her eyes. She drew a long breath and said, "That was . . . you shouldn't have said that, Matt. I mean, the last part. It . . . well, it kind of spoils things. You're entitled to think it, but you shouldn't say it. You make me feel like a tramp, and I don't like it."

I said, "Better to feel it now than after it's too late, sweetheart. Now you know how my low-down mind is running. I'll use you if I can and I'll lay you if I can, and if you get messed up in other ways, or even killed, I'll hoist one drink in your memory and go on to the next job."

"And the next woman?"

"Sure."

She laughed softly. Her dark glasses reflected the beach behind me as she looked at me. "You're very tough, aren't you?"

"It's a tough racket."

"There were flowers on the grave," she said quietly. "Fresh flowers."

I stared at her. "What grave?"

"Winifred's grave. In a little village cemetery in southern France. The gatekeeper said the tall man who left the money for the flowers had tears in his eyes. That couldn't be you, of course, Matt. You're the tough guy who lays them and leaves them without a backward glance." She smiled gently. "My husband thinks you're a murderer. He was very fond of his little sister. She was probably the only human being, besides himself, that he ever really cared for. He thinks you married her for her inheritance and did away with her. We were both sure of it, when we saw the lengths to which you'd gone to make it look like a simple car accident. We learned you were coming here. . ."

"How?" My voice sounded rusty.

"The lawyers got a forwarding address from some government department. We, Kenneth and I, decided that it would be best for me to fly out and be waiting to tackle you alone. I was to see if I couldn't get you to incriminate yourself somehow." Her smile widened and turned faintly bitter. "Of course, our motives aren't quite unselfish, Matt. There's a good deal of money involved, nearly half a million dollars apiece, and my husband has already run through or obligated most of his share. If we can prove you murdered Winifred, then of course you can't benefit from your crime, and her legacy will revert to the estate, meaning Kenneth and me."

I had to clear my throat before I could speak again. "Just who the hell are you?" I asked.

"Why," she said, still smiling brightly, "why, I'm your sister-in-law, darling. I'm Isobel Marner."

Chapter Eleven

THE UNEXPECTEDNESS OF it kind of took my breath away. Since my divorce several years ago, I've been strictly a non-family man. I'm not used to having relatives walk up and introduce themselves in the middle of a job, especially relatives by a marriage that was never performed. To cover up, I reached for the white purse on the table.

"Do you mind?"

Isobel had started to protest, but she laughed instead. "No, of course not. Go right ahead. Is this what they call a frisk?"

I said, "No, a frisk is lots more fun. My God, the junk you women carry in those suitcases!"

Actually, the purse was reasonably uncluttered and quite innocent of surprises. There was nothing in it you wouldn't expect to find in the purse of any modern woman who used cigarettes and cosmetics, or if there was, it was well enough camouflaged that I could afford to let myself be fooled by it. The small, lady-type wallet held a California driver's license and various other cards issued to (Mrs.) Isobel Caroline Marner, 1286 Seaview Drive, San Francisco. I remembered that the letter from the lawyers had also originated in San Francisco.

"My passport is in my suitcase, at the hotel," she said. "I'll show it to you when we get back, if you like."

"Why a passport to come to Hawaii, a state of the U.S.A.?" I asked suspiciously.

She took back her purse, smiling. "I told you. We went to France to investigate Winnie's death; naturally I had a passport. And I didn't know where you might lead me from here so I brought it along." She hesitated. "Now you might let me look in your wallet, just to make us even."

I said, "It wouldn't do you any good. You know my
80

name. Your lawyers seem to've tracked down as much address as I've got. What else do you want, a card saying Secret Agent?"

She laughed. "I guess I'm being naïve. But I only have your word for it."

"That's right."

"You could be just about anybody," she persisted. "Anybody with a gun."

"That's right."

"You're not being much help, Matt."

"That's right," I said. "Let's order some lunch. I'm hungry."

After we'd given our orders and the waitress had departed, Isobel stubbed out her cigarette and looked at me. "May I ask just one question?"

"Go ahead."

"Assuming you're telling the truth, and you are an undercover operative of some kind for the U.S. Government, was Winnie one, too?"

I said, "I can't answer that. If she was, it would come under the heading of classified information, wouldn't it?"

"You've told me what you are. If you're telling the truth. Isn't that classified, too?"

"You kind of tricked it out of me, catching me with a gun out," I said. "I had to give you a reasonable explanation, to avoid damaging publicity. We're allowed to use the truth judiciously in such cases; we're not one of the outfits that make a holy fetish of security, thank God. But that doesn't mean I can lay the whole operation open to you, just to satisfy your girlish curiosity."

"It's a little more than girlish curiosity." Isobel's voice was sharp. "I mean, if she was an agent, too, and you were working together, and she got killed in the line of duty, then maybe—"

"Maybe what?"

"Maybe you weren't really married. Maybe you were just pretending to be. Maybe it was just, what do you call it in your work, a cover? And in that case—"

She was a smart woman. I grinned at her across the table. "In that case, you and your Kenneth would be home free, wouldn't you? No marriage, no inheritance for me. Shucks, and I was just starting to feel so rich, too!"

Isobel didn't smile. "Unfortunately for us, it isn't quite that simple. Whether or not you were married to her, there's still the will; she was legally entitled to leave her money to any man she chose, husband or no. . . ."

This was all taking us pretty far from what had brought me to Hawaii, but of course I couldn't say so. To act uninterested would have been suspicious. It would have indicated that I had more important things on my mind than half a million dollars.

"Wait a minute!" I said. "What will are we talking about now? From a letter I got and from what you've told me, I gather that the old man, Philip Grant Marner or whatever his name was, willed his estate to his kids Kenneth and Winifred. Is that right?"

"Yes, of course. And Winnie left her share to you, in a document mailed from France about a week before she died. Didn't you know?"

I thought of a small girl with silver-blonde hair who'd never talked much about herself. My voice sounded odd and far away when I spoke: "No, I didn't know. I didn't even know the kid had money. She never told me."

"Of course you'd say that."

I looked up, and drew a long breath, and managed a grin. "Sure. I'm a born liar. You can't trust a word I say."

Isobel said grimly, "And you can get that sentimental look off your face. Maybe Winnie was fond of you and maybe she wasn't—I wouldn't know about that—but she didn't pass her inheritance on to you because of your sex appeal. She did it to spite me and to protect the older brother she idolized."

"Protect him?" I said. "By keeping him from getting her share of the dough if she died? That's protection?"

"Yes. Because she knew he was almost broke, and she thought I would leave him if he could no longer support me properly. And in her opinion, my leaving Kenneth would be the biggest break of his life. She hated me, and she had the theory, I'm sure, that without me to drag him down, he'd manage to make a man of himself somehow." Isobel shrugged. "Well, that was one girl's opinion. We always did disagree about what was good for Kenneth, Winnie and I. I managed to win that battle; that's why she went away and took a government job." Isobel smiled. "She never let us know what kind of job it was, except that it involved a lot of traveling. But I can guess, can't I? Just as I can guess that you weren't really married."

There was a little break while the waitress served our lunches; then I said, "If there's a will, what difference does our matrimonial status make?"

"Wills can be broken, darling. What did they call this fish?"

"*Mahimahi.* Something local," I said. "Is it any good?"

"Fabulous. Look, they've got almonds in the sauce! And if we did decide to try to break Winnie's last will and testament, charging duress or incompetence or something, we'd probably have a better chance if you'd been just casual lovers rather than man and wife." She regarded me coolly across the table. "And, of course, if you're not what you claim to be, and if you did murder Winnie after all. . . . Well, as I said, that's what I was hoping to prove when I came out here."

"And now?" I asked.

She smiled slowly. "Now I'll have to use another approach, darling. Because, to be perfectly honest, after meeting you and talking with you, I don't really think you killed her. And I don't really think her will can be broken. So there's only one thing left for me to do, isn't there? All I can do is throw myself on your mercy, my dear brother-in-law, and hope that somehow I can make you feel generous toward me. Well, toward Kenneth and me."

There was a little silence. "Half a million is a lot of generosity," I said at last, watching her closely. It didn't seem like real money we were discussing, the kind you could pay bills with or use in the Coke machine.

"Oh, I don't expect you to renounce it all," she said

calmly. "But you're obviously not a man who thinks too much about money; it doesn't mean a great deal to you. Apparently you've got a good salary and your tastes aren't too expensive. You could be generous and pass up, say, half the legacy and never notice it. And it would mean a great deal . . . a very great deal to us. To me." She looked down and found a cigarette and did her nervous fast-draw trick with the lighter once more. Without looking up, she said, "You said something about . . . about finding a use for me, Matt."

"In bed or out," I agreed. "I did say something like that, didn't I?"

She blew smoke toward the nearest palm tree. "In bed is easy," she said, quite unruffled. "If that's all you want, let's get back to the hotel. For a quarter of a million, darling, I'd sleep with the devil himself."

"Thanks," I said. "There's nothing like making a man feel wanted for himself alone, I always say. What else would you do for approximately two hundred and fifty grand?"

"Just about anything," she said steadily. "Just name it and tell me how. I don't have much experience with your kind of melodrama, but I'm bright and willing to learn." She was silent briefly, and went on, "I know I'm revealing myself as a dreadfully mercenary person, but don't rub my nose in it any harder than you have to, Matt. I do have a certain amount of pride."

"Sorry," I said, and meant it. "As a matter of fact, I think I can find a use for you outside the obvious one. How much risk are you willing to run for a quarter of a million?"

She said any amount. They always say that, the ones who've never been shot at in their lives.

Chapter Twelve

OUR MAN FRANCIS, alias Bill Menander, was still on the job when we squeezed ourselves into my rented Sprite and departed from the hotel parking lot with some pretty sports-car sound effects. I heard Isobel laugh.

"What's funny?" I asked.

"This car. It's hardly the inconspicuous vehicle one would expect a hush-hush operative to choose, except on TV."

"Maybe that's just why I picked it," I said. "What's your feeling on the subject of porpoises?"

"What?"

"Porpoises," I said. "Large, fishy-looking mammals with superior intelligence. According to one theory, when the human race finally succeeds in blowing itself up, the porpoises will take over, if there's anything left to take. I ask because I learned at the aquarium that there's a park way out around Diamond Head somewhere that has trained porpoises putting on acts."

I glanced in the mirror. The Datsun was right behind us as we headed out Kalakaua Avenue, named after one of the Hawaiian kings who came after they'd run out of Kamehamehas. The sidewalks were crowded with pretty young girls in muu-muus and young military characters in uniform. Just one transport-load had given Waikiki a very martial air.

I said, "For various reasons, not all ichthyological, I'd kind of like to drive out that way."

Isobel said dubiously, "Well, I'm not really terribly fond of fish, except to eat. That goes for mammals masquerading as fish. However . . ." She hesitated. "We're being followed, aren't we?"

"That's right."

"And you want to run the man around a bit?"

"More or less. He hasn't had his exercise for the day. I'd hate to let him get soft and lazy."

"Then by all means let's go look at porpoises." Isobel hesitated, and said in a different tone, "Matt?"

"Yes?"

"If . . . if I'm going to help you, if we're going to work together, shouldn't I know a few things? Like who that man behind us is, and whom he represents?"

It wasn't an unexpected question. She'd asked more or less the same thing last night and I'd put her off; now I had to make the decision for good. I had a three-way choice. I could take her into my confidence and tell her the whole truth, as far as I knew it, about Monk's treachery and my plans to combat it. Or I could stick to my official cover story, tailoring it to fit the new situation. Or I could continue to play the security gambit, even if it meant getting nasty.

Stalling, I said, "I can tell you who he probably is. I figure there's about a fifty-percent chance he's the guy who clobbered you last night."

"That still doesn't really identify him," she protested.

"No," I said. "It doesn't, does it?"

"He could be what you claim to be, a U.S. agent."

"He certainly could," I said.

"And you could be a Russian spy."

"No question about it," I agreed. The decision had kind of made itself as we talked, and I went on, "But you know one thing I am for sure."

She frowned slightly. "What's that?"

"Santa Claus," I said. "Santa Claus with a bagful of money, which I'm willing to divide with you in return for services rendered. Services, Mrs. Marner. Not questions. Is my signal getting through, Mrs. Marner? Do you receive me clearly?"

I saw the muscles tighten along her jaw. Her voice was small and stiff when she spoke, "You don't have to be offensive, Matt."

I said, "And you don't have to be inquisitive, Isobel. Just do as you're told and keep your questions to yourself and we'll get along just fine." I glanced at her. "Now you're mad," I said. I shrugged. "Okay. It was just a wild idea of mine, anyway. I'll take you back to the hotel."

She caught my arm as I started to shift gears for the turn. "No," she said.

"Make up your mind," I said. "This is the point of no return, as the fly-boys call it."

"You're an infuriating man," she said. She drew a long breath. "I dote on infuriating men. I think. Keep driving."

I drove on, feeling kind of ashamed of myself for cracking the whip and of her for letting me get away with it, but at least we'd settled the point. When you came right down to it, I couldn't very well have told her I was using her to create a diversion for a girl named Jill; and any other answer would have involved too many complicated lies. . . .

The porpoises were kind of scary. I don't really like to see bright fishes, even when they're mammals. It doesn't seem quite natural. It was just as well for my peace of mind, therefore, that the cast included a couple of extremely pretty native-type girls in sarongs. They helped take my mind off the intellectual attainments of the dolphins.

After the show, we went back to the parking lot where we'd left the car. It was a rambling area carved out of a hillside with a lot of grass and bushes and trees. I closed the car door on Isobel and leaned down to speak to her through the open window.

"Okay, here's where you get your first lesson in secret agentry. There's a very useful technique known as patient waiting. Let's see how good you are at it. I'll be back."

I walked around the car, bent over as if to get in, and opened and closed the door loudly. Crouching there, I checked my gun and my little drug kit. Then, keeping low, I dove into the bushes, made my way through them, and circled wide up the hill. The approach was easy. He was sitting with his back to the slope. Every so often he'd lean forward impatiently to look around the tree where he was parked so he could see the red sports car, but it never occurred to him to look behind. I slipped between the cars and stuck my gun in his ear.

He gave a sudden start and was very quiet. "Eric?"

"That's right," I said. "Eric. Keep looking straight ahead. What's your code name, punk?" I knew it, of course, but I wasn't supposed to, so I had to let him make it official. He hesitated. "Come on, come on. We're colleagues, aren't we? It's all in the family."

"Francis," he whispered.

"And what name are you operating under, Francis?"

"Menander. Bill Menander. Look, I don't know what you're trying to do. . . ."

"That's right, you don't know. But I do. And I'll be bighearted and tell you. I'm trying to impress upon you that it's a dangerous life you've chosen, and that you don't want to take unnecessary risks and make it more dangerous. Understand? Now, me I don't worry about. The day I let a punk like you worry me will really be the day. Play any kind of games you like with me. Or try. But the lady gets left strictly alone. No more searches. No more gun barrels alongside the head. No more anything."

"But—"

I didn't let him interrupt. "If I see her being followed, if I spot a tap on her phone, if I stumble on a mike in her room, if there's the slightest sign that somebody's been looking through her stuff again or reading her mail, guess what'll happen?" He didn't speak. I nudged him with the gun. "I spoke to you, punk. Guess!"

"What . . . what will happen?"

"You'll die," I said. "That's what will happen."

"But if somebody else . . ."

I said harshly, "That's your worry, not mine. The lady is a relative of mine. Just a relative, nothing more. She came to Hawaii to have a good time. She's going to have a good time without being bothered by a lot of U.S. undercover creeps. You keep them out of her hair, hear?"

"But I'm not responsible for. . . What if I can't help . . . ?"

"Then I just won't be able to help, either. I'll just have to kill you, punk."

He said with sudden strength, "You're bluffing. You wouldn't dare. . ."

"The name is Eric, punk. Ask around. Check with the Monk. He'll tell you what I don't dare, and it won't take any time at all. The list is very short, punk. Very short indeed!"

He licked his lips. "Don't call me punk!"

"Why the hell not? You are a punk, just a crummy, bleeding-heart punk with a big mouth. I've heard stories about the kids the Monk's been recruiting out here lately, shooting their mouths off all over the Islands. Like that kookie blonde female who thought she was Mata Hari with wings on. Wanting me to weep with her for the woes of Asia, for Christ's sake!"

He cleared his throat. "According to the record, you've been known to talk out of turn, too. On the same subject."

I said, "Yeah, and I'm damned ashamed of the company it puts me in. It's enough to make a man recant on the spot." I poked him with the gun. "But you pass the word. The lady's out of bounds. Or there comes a large hole in the head. Put your elbow on the window-sill. . . . Up with it, punk! You try my patience, you really do!"

"What . . . what are you going to do to me?"

"I'm going to put you to sleep for about two hours. When you wake up, you can have a lot of fun trying to find us again. It will be good experience for you. Happy dreams."

I slipped the needle into him before he could protest, and gave him the dose. He turned his head against orders to look at me at last, wide-eyed and panicky. He started to speak, but whatever he'd been about to say, he never got out.

I caught him as he fell forward against the steering wheel and arranged him in the seat with his chin on his chest. I reached past him to get a straw hat with a flowered band that was lying beside him on the seat. I set this well forward on his head, covering most of his face, so that he looked like a man taking a nap, which he was.

Isobel received me coolly when I returned to the Sprite, acting as if she had no interest in where I'd been or what I'd done, but her indifference faded as we drove past the Datsun and she saw the man behind the wheel with his hat over his face.

"Did you . . . did you kill him?"

I said, "Bloodthirsty, aren't you? No, I didn't kill him. I gave him a couple of hours' sleep, that's all, a perfectly harmless injection." I glanced at my watch. "Well, we've got about an hour and a half to get to the airport, which is clear on the other side of Honolulu. I hope you're a fast packer. We'll keep our rooms at the hotel, if you can stand the expense. Just take enough clothes for a couple of days. I hope we can get seats on the damn plane."

She said tartly, "I won't spoil it by asking where we're going. You're having too much fun keeping me in suspense."

We talked no more, driving back to the Halekulani. I guess she was still mad at me. As for me, I guess I felt kind of guilty about what I'd just done to her. Because Monk wouldn't believe that she was merely one of my more attractive female relations. He'd think that story was too ridiculous to waste a moment on. And he certainly wouldn't heed my warning to leave her alone. On the contrary, I figured, he'd take it as a cue to give her special attention, and there was no telling what form it would take.

Well, that was, after all, what the woman was getting paid for, and well paid: attracting the special attentions of the Monk away from another girl, a girl who had work to do and was, I hoped, busily engaged in doing it.

Chapter Thirteen

WE CAUGHT THE late afternoon plane to Kahului with a few minutes to spare and even managed to get seats together. Taking off, we had a good view of Honolulu harbor from the air and caught a glimpse of the naval installations at Pearl Harbor to the west. I would have liked to know more about those. After all, that was where the Japs had struck in 1941. It wasn't inconceivable that the Chinese had hit on the notion of perpetuating a good old Oriental custom, with Monk's help.

We straightened out over the ocean and flew along in a more or less easterly direction past Waikiki and Diamond Head, discovering that what had looked like a solid mountain from the ground was actually an extinct volcano with a definite, hollow crater. There were more boats out than there had been that morning, but the seas around Oahu were still by no means crowded.

"Matt?" Isobel's voice indicated that, having punished me sufficiently, she was willing to stop being mad at me.

I turned from the window, reminding myself that I was still playing a role. My cover as an agent in disgrace killing time in the tropics hadn't, as far as I knew, greatly impressed anybody who really mattered—I'd never been as sold on it as the man who'd thought of it—but I couldn't just drop it without warning the opposition that I had something new and tricky in mind. And as a gentleman of enforced leisure, setting out to spend a couple of glorious Hawaiian days, and nights, in the company of an attractive woman, I wouldn't normally be paying a great deal of attention to the view.

Isobel asked, "Did we . . . did we make it, Matt?"

I frowned. "Did we make what?"

"Well, you *were* trying to lose them, weren't you? I mean, drugging that boy and dashing for the plane!"

I laughed. "Isobel, I'm afraid you're an optimist. You

91

don't think that kid was the only one, do you? Pardon
me for flattering myself a bit, but to keep watch on an
old curly wolf like yours truly, you'd generally figure on
using your shadows at least two deep, maybe three."

"You mean there's somebody else—"

"There's a hook-nosed gent four seats to the rear, a
dark man in a dark business suit with a briefcase. I
spotted him at the hotel this morning, using binoculars
industriously. Apparently he's taken over the watch
from our sleeping young friend. And you can bet there'll
be somebody waiting to back him up when we get to
Kahului, in case we should manage to ditch him, too."

"Then what in the world was the point of—" She
checked herself, and held up her hand quickly. "All
right, all right! Don't bite. I withdraw the question. Just
give the orders, Master, and they shall be obeyed. But
may I ask where Kahului is, since I'll presumably learn
that much when we land, anyway?"

"It's on the island of Maui," I said. Isobel looked
blank. I grinned. "You should have done some home-
work before coming out here. Maui is the second island
down from Oahu, just beyond Molokai. In addition to
Kahului, where the airport is, and various other com-
munities, it's got an old town on it called Lahaina. The
whalers used to anchor in the roadstead and come ashore
to get drunk and cohabit—I'm quoting the book—with
the native girls, who were apparently both beautiful and
willing. But the missionaries came along and spoiled
everything. Now there are several luxury hotels just up
the coast. You can still get all the liquor you want, I
gather, but these days you have to bring your own girl."

Isobel's eyes narrowed slightly. "And I suppose we've
got a reservation at one of these hotels?"

"That is more or less correct, ma'am," I said. "I
called around while you were packing and found a place
that wasn't full. But the word is reservations, plural.
Two rooms. Just as chaste as can be, ma'am."

She regarded me for a moment, and smiled slowly.
"All right, Matt. Thank you. I didn't mean to be stuffy,
but I don't believe it was part of the final agreement.

. . . Of course I did say I'd do anything. But I don't like to be taken for granted, in that respect. I want to be asked."

"I'll ask," I said. "Don't worry, if it becomes indicated, I'll surely ask. But regardless of how many beds actually get slept in by how many people, I'd like us to present a nice immoral image to the world. I hope you don't mind."

She shrugged. "Well, I'm not quite the society whore my husband likes to tell me I am, when he's in a mood to enumerate his many afflictions. On the other hand, I'm hardly pure enough to qualify as a Vestal Virgin tending the sacred flame, or whatever they tended. So by all means, let's tear my poor reputation to tatters, what's left of it."

On acquaintance, she showed a kind of humorous honesty that tended to overcome the first impression created by her arrogant mannerisms and snooty good looks. I was annoyed to find myself beginning to like her. It was about time, I told myself, that I learned to keep my affectionate nature under control. I was an agent on a mission, not a friendly puppy out for a romp. Still, a little precautionary briefing wouldn't hurt me and might help her.

"One suggestion," I said. "Or maybe you could call it a warning. I don't know how this will break. But you might just possibly wind up in an awkward spot with people asking questions. I don't expect it, but it could happen. If it does, I think you'll be best off if you just give them your straight sister-in-law act, without frills."

She asked calmly, "And what do I say about you, Matt? If I'm asked?"

"As far as I'm concerned," I said, "you can tell them anything you want. Anything you know."

She laughed. "That's very generous of you. Since you've been very careful to see that I know hardly anything."

"You may be grateful for that," I said. "The less you know—the less you appear to know—the easier time you're likely to have. I suggest, as a guideline, the following story: you came to Hawaii to find the other heir to the Marner millions—well, million. Your husband doesn't know you're here. He wouldn't approve, of course, but you were desperate, you saw grim poverty ahead for you and Kenneth, and you hoped you could persuade your unknown brother-in-law to share the inherited wealth. It developed that you could, by falling in with certain lewd suggestions. Well, what your husband doesn't know won't hurt him, and for a quarter of a million, to paraphrase your own words, you'd spend a weekend with the devil in the hottest corner of hell. That's your story. Stick to it and don't elaborate on it at all."

She nodded. "It should be easy enough to remember."

"Don't kid yourself. Nothing's easy, when you're being interrogated. Just keep in mind that you simply don't know there's anything mysterious going on. You don't know that I'm anything but a rather crude and common character who married your husband's impossible sister, now fortunately dead, whose taste in men was always deplorable. You have no idea that I brought you to Maui for any purpose but to collect what you'd promised me, in a somewhat more intimate atmosphere than that of Honolulu. You're even a little insulted at the notion that I might have had an ulterior motive. Okay?"

"In other words, I play very dumb," she said. She hesitated. "Are they . . . apt to beat me?"

"To a bloody pulp," I said cheerfully. "That should at least keep you from being bored, Duchess. You were complaining of boredom, remember?"

She made a face at me. "It seems like a long time ago. Matt?"

"Yes."

"There's one question I have to ask. If I continue to go along with this, if I do what you tell me—"

"You want to know about the payoff? I don't know what it would take to make it legal, but if you want to write something, I'll be glad to sign it."

A little anger showed in her eyes. "That isn't what I was going to ask, Matt. I don't think about money *all* the time. I'm a pretty good judge of men—I've only made one bad mistake in my life—and I'm fairly sure that if you can, you'll pay off. I'll gamble on that, without any papers that probably wouldn't mean anything legally, anyway."

I said, "Thanks. Then what's bugging you?"

"I want to know, if I do everything you ask, will I be a traitor to my country? I mean, I still have no proof of who you are."

. I looked at her for a moment, but her expression told me nothing. I said, "Make up your mind, Isobel. Either you're a good judge of men or you aren't."

She shook her head. "It isn't that easy, where politics is concerned. I mean, a man may be quite dependable in every other respect, but he'll still do dreadful things if he gets it into his head that he's saving the world or something."

I said, "It's still a stupid damn question and I'm ashamed of you for asking it."

"Why is it stupid?" she demanded. "I think it's fairly important, myself. I'm not the greatest patriot in the world, but just the same—"

"Important, sure," I interrupted, "but look whom you're asking! You're not going to get an answer from me: not an answer you can trust. So all you're really doing is asking me to give your conscience a tranquillizer, so you can save yourself the trouble of looking at me and deciding for yourself whether I'm an immaculate Patrick Henry or a dirty Benedict Arnold. Well, to hell with that, Duchess. It's your conscience. Don't ask me to talk to it. You tell it what it wants to hear."

She said sharply, "You're not being much help!"

"Hell, it's nothing I can help you with, and you know it. Suppose I were to tell you that the fate of the U.S. depends on our efforts, and that if we're successful you'll be a national heroine and get your face on a postage stamp. That's what you want to hear, isn't it? But if I say it, will you believe it? If you do, you're better at fooling yourself than I think you are."

There was a little silence; then she laughed. "You're either a very honest man or a very clever one."

"Can't I be both?" I asked plaintively. Neither of us said anything for a while, and the subject kind of died by default. At last I pointed out the window. "Look, there's Molokai already."

"That's the leper colony, isn't it?"

I said, mechanically, "You're not supposed to call it leprosy these days. It's Hansen's disease. That makes it much more respectable."

We watched the island approach. Down below, I saw a white powerboat smashing through the trade-wind chop at a pretty good clip, judging by the wake. It could be a speedboat belonging to a man called Monk, I reflected, although he was supposed to pick night for the run as a rule. It could have aboard a girl called Jill, and if this had been a TV show she'd have been equipped with a convenient electronic gadget that would have allowed me to track her in my midget sub, if I'd had a midget sub.

Unfortunately, we were dealing with a smart and experienced man, not a TV villain. Asking Jill to plant a tracking device on the Monk would have been equivalent to asking her to commit suicide. He would have thought of all such logical possibilities, and he'd be ready for them all, somehow. I wasn't going to beat the Monk with gadgets. With his experience with explosives and detonators, he was a much better gadget man than I was.

The only way I'd trip him up would be by doing something quite untechnical and illogical. I still hadn't figured out just what.

Chapter Fourteen

WE GOT A VIEW of the flat western end of Molokai with its geometrical red-earth pineapple fields, but the mountainous eastern end was pretty well covered by the clouds that tend to collect over higher elevations in the Islands. On Oahu, I'd already discovered, you can stand in Waikiki in bright sunshine, and watch it raining like hell up on the Pali. High up among the mountains of Kauai there's supposed to be a rain-soaked region that's the wettest spot on earth. Molokai was apparently no exception to this weather rule.

The visibility, angle, and distance were poor for the particular stretch of windward coast in which I was interested. Well, I could hardly expect Hawaiian Airlines to fly reconnaissance for me, although it would have been convenient. I did, however, get a chance to observe that, as the maps had indicated, the next stretch of water wasn't nearly as wide as the first one we'd crossed.

Then we were coming up on the island of Maui with a small mountain range at one end and a tremendous, cloud-capped volcanic peak at the other: Haleakala, the House of the Sun. I'd seen ten-thousand-foot mountains before, plenty of them, but mainly in the western U.S., where they rise out of country that's a mile high to start with. This one came straight up out of the sea.

The backup man was waiting for us at the Kahului Airport. My hawk-faced shadow with the briefcase was off the plane before us, but he stopped inside the terminal to light a cigarette, timing it so that his match flared just as Isobel and I walked past. I scanned the room surreptitiously and spotted the man for whom we'd been pointed out. He was lounging casually by the windows.

This was another one we had no record of—another of Monk's unlisted reserves—a big, golden-brown, good-looking Hawaiian character with a red-flowered sport shirt hanging outside white duck pants and bare brown feet stuck into leather sandals. Although well into his thirties, he had the friendly, boyish look that's characteristic of the race, but I didn't put too much faith in it. History says that while they were generally just about the sweetest people on earth, they could turn very mean upon occasion, as Captain Cook discovered. They killed him on a beach a couple of islands away from this one when he tried to get tough with them. Then, because he'd been considered a god of sorts, they cleaned the flesh off his bones and passed them around for good luck.

I spoke to Isobel as we walked through the building. "Remember that I called ahead from Honolulu. That means the opposition has had plenty of time to make any preparations they like in our rooms and in the car we're picking up here at the airport. So don't say anything in either place you don't want anybody to overhear."

Her eyes were bright. "You mean they could even have bugged the car? How quaint! That's the right word, isn't it, bugged?"

"That's right," I said. "Bugged. Now if you really prefer to be chaste this evening, I think you'd better have a headache. We'll stop in town to get you some aspirin for it. It's probably a result of that blow on the head last night. It's making you feel pretty bad, and you're sorry but you'd like to go to bed early, alone."

"But . . ." She glanced at me sharply, a little disconcerted. Obviously she hadn't expected me to be quite so considerate of her virtue. "Oh. I see. You have something you want to do tonight. Alone."

"Check."

She moved her shoulders. "Yes, Master. To hear is to obey. . . . That beach-boy type over by the windows. Could he be the man you said might be waiting for us here?"

"He could, but we're not supposed to know it. At least I don't think we are. And you're not supposed to be clever and observant, Mrs. Marner. You're just a stupid, self-centered, society bitch and don't you forget it. Bright people get hurt."

She laughed. "All right, Matt. I'm warned again." Her momentary resentment had faded. She took my arm, walking close to me. When she spoke again, her voice was mischievous: "It's really too bad you're going to be so busy. I just happened to bring along a very pretty nightie—quite by accident, of course."

I grinned. "I've seen your damn nighties, doll. I'm the guy who cleans up your room nights, remember? For your own sake, just stick to the script, please. I want to keep you out of this as much as possible. So don't louse things up by getting irresistible at the wrong time."

Her fingers pressed lightly on my arm. "Well, at least it's reassuring to know that you think I can."

The car they gave us was a reasonably new Ford sedan, equipped with every gadget to make life miserable for an old sports car hand like me. The power steering would throw you into the ditch before you knew you'd turned the wheel; the power brakes would hurl you through the windshield before you knew you'd found the pedal; and the automatic transmission would run you through a stoplight before you even thought of touching the accelerator. Detroit makes the most comfortable and reliable cars in the world, for the price, but they're designed for people who want the car to do the driving. After a stint in Europe, I was accustomed to docile, obedient little vehicles humbly ready to serve me, not great arrogant mechanical monsters with minds of their own.

The hooknosed man had apparently turned me over to his relief. I saw him go to a parked car and ride off without a backward glance, but the golden boy was right behind us in a battered old jeep as we drove into town—well, let's call it driving. I found that the only way to beat the hydraulic gremlins at their own game was to keep one foot ready on the instant brake to cancel the mistakes of the instant gears. This made our progress a bit jerky, but it saved a lot of wear and tear on telephone poles and pedestrians.

"Are you doing that for fun, or are you just learning to drive?" Isobel asked as we took off impulsively after buying aspirin. She patted her hair into place and tightened her seat belt. "When you get tired of it, I'll be glad to take over."

"I hope you're not going to turn out to be one of these competent damn females," I said. "I like the helpless type much better. Anyway, I've handled everything from a gull-wing Mercedes to an Army six-by-six; I'm going to lick this Supermarket Special if it takes all night."

"Well, you're not doing my headache one bit of good."

"So take an aspirin, doll," I said. "That's what we bought them for."

Having established, if anyone was listening electronically, that the course of true love wasn't running quite smoothly, we drove south across the narrow waist of the island and up along the curving leeward shore under a clear blue sky. Behind us loomed the giant mass of Haleakala, still wreathed in clouds from about five thousand feet up. I gather you can see the top occasionally, but you have to get up early in the morning to do it.

The coast highway was a two-lane blacktop road flanked by feathery trees, identified in the guide book by the local name of *kiawe*. They looked to me just like plain old Texas mesquites that had got plenty of vitamins. I didn't stop in the historic little coastal village of Lahaina that I'd described to Isobel, but I did drive through slowly enough to make sure that, as I'd expected, there was a long dock holding pleasure and fishing boats of every description. At least one of them ought to be for hire, I reflected, and Molokai was just around the corner, nautically speaking.

As a matter of fact, the island of lepers was clearly visible across the water to the north as we drove on. To my landlubber eyes, it looked like a long and risky small-boat voyage, and it was a pretty obvious gambit anyway, but I might as well play at it until something better turned up. I could at least go through the motions of making the arrangements. That would give the golden boy and his hawkfaced friend something interesting to report—and the more interest I aroused here, the less would be left over for Jill, wherever she was.

Then we were passing a group of elaborate resort hotels and a beautifully manicured golf course where athletic characters, male and female, were getting lots of healthful exercise in little electric carts. The shoreline got more rugged as we continued north until we spotted a hill overlooking a lovely, sandy cove. Spilling down the sides of the hill was a rambling hostelry that somebody had obviously used a lot of expense and ingenuity in

designing; a little less might have been more in keeping
with the spirit of the Islands.

But this was a high-class joint that didn't intend to be
mistaken for anything else. As we drove up, I saw Isobel
break out the repair kit and attend to her hair and lipstick. She lit a cigarette in her quick, nervous way and
dropped the lighter back into her purse.

"I'm about ready for a drink," she said. "I'd like a
drink before I change for dinner."

"I get the message," I said. "No further repetition is
necessary. We'll get you a drink. We might even get me
one, too. I'm going to need it if you're planning to have
a headache all evening."

She said, "It's not my fault if I got hit on the head
by a mysterious prowler. . . ."

We carried this bickering act into the hotel bar, and
then to the rooms, which did not adjoin but were several
doors apart: the best I'd been able to do on such short
notice. I made a perfunctory gesture toward seeing that
she was settled in hers, and started to leave. She called
me back.

"Matt."

"Yes?"

She walked past me and closed the door and turned
to face me. "I really do have a dreadful headache, darling," she said. "You might sympathize a little instead of
acting as if I were just trying to be difficult." She seemed
very sincere; she was really a pretty good actress.

I hesitated, figuring what would sound best to the
eavesdroppers, if any. Finally I said, "I'm sorry. I'm a
selfish louse, baby. Kick me."

She laughed and came up to me, took my face in her
hands, and kissed me on the mouth—but what had
started out as a friendly peck of reconciliation quickly
grew, under her deliberate and expert guidance, into
something considerably more passionate and breathless.
This was obviously not part of the plan I'd laid out for
her. I was sure of it when her arms went around my
neck, and various other things happened, all quite disturbing to a man who'd been celibate for weeks.

"You bitch!" I whispered fondly, freeing myself enough to speak.

Both malice and mischief showed in her face. She pressed her cheek against mine and spoke in my ear: "What's the matter, can't you keep your mind on your work, Mr. Secret Agent? You're going to be busy tonight, remember? And I've got such a terrible headache. Simply awful. You said so yourself."

There was no real reason for me to put up with this nonsense. I mean, I'd been noble in Honolulu, but a young girl trying to impersonate Mata Hari was one thing. A grown woman playing sex games was something else. I'd generously offered her an excuse to stay reasonably clear of the action. If she didn't want to use it, that was her business.

I said harshly, reaching for her, "Sabotage is what it is. I told you not to get irresistible, damn you!"

Her voice mocked me. "Remember the microphones, darling."

"To hell with the mikes."

I took hold of her and pulled her hard against me, doing some minor violence to the integrity of her costume as I kissed her again. This brought a quick protest.

"Matt, don't! You'll ruin my—"

"And to hell with that, too," I snapped. "You should have thought of it before you started this. I warned you to go easy, doll, but you had to prove how sexy you are. Now just come over to the bed and get raped like a good girl."

She said angrily, resisting me, "I loathe masterful men! I can't stand them! I told you. I want to be asked."

"Will you please step over to the bed and get raped, Mrs. Marner, ma'am?"

"That's better," she breathed. "That's much better. Yes, Mr. Helm, sir, if you'll give me a moment to slip out of a few clothes, I'll be delighted to step over to the bed and get raped."

Chapter Fifteen

LATER, WE HAD ANOTHER drink out on the hotel terrace—well, on one of the several terraces jutting from the seaward hillside like random bookshelves from a wall. It was getting dark and the bathers had deserted the beach below. An attendant in swim trunks was putting half a dozen small boats to bed. That is, he was taking down the colorfully striped, triangular little sails and hauling the tiny vessels out on the sand. They looked like the same kind of sailing planks, twelve or fourteen feet long, that I'd seen used by kids in the surf off Waikiki.

Where we were, on the western shore of the island, the trade winds couldn't hit us directly, but far out beyond the lee of the land the ocean looked rough and choppy in the growing dusk. There was a low island out there in line with the sunset: that would be Lanai. To the north was the brooding, cloud-wrapped mass of Molokai. Between here and there, according to the chart I'd studied, was something called the Pailolo Channel, ten miles wide and some hundred and thirty fathoms deep.

I'd once, long ago, been exposed to a bit of rudimentary seamanship in the line of duty. A course in basic boat-handling had been required at the time, since we were operating along the coasts of Europe, and reliable nautical help wasn't always to be had. I still remembered that one fathom was equal to six feet. Not that it mattered. You can drown in six inches of water if you put your mind to it.

"Is it permitted to disturb the Master at his meditations?" Isobel asked respectfully.

I looked up. "Only for matters of the utmost importance."

"I just wanted to say that I'm sorry."

I grinned. "Now there's a way to make a man feel he's given real satisfaction. The dame regrets, yet."

"I didn't mean that." Isobel didn't smile. "I was merely apologizing for being a perverse bitch. I know you were being nice and trying to protect me as much as possible, and I do appreciate it."

"Sure," I said. "Well, let's figure how much damage has been done. We'll have to assume that they overheard what we said, but even if they didn't, it doesn't take a genius to figure out that a wench who's in bed with the guy before the bellboy's even made it back to the desk obviously isn't a wench who's reluctantly keeping her part of a distasteful bargain. So that story's out. What's the matter?"

"Nothing," she said. "I didn't say anything." There was a certain coolness in her voice.

I laughed at her. "I know, you'd rather I put it in a more dignified way, Duchess. Well, I'm sorry, but I'm trying to look at it through the eyes of the opposition. You'll never make them believe you're an unwilling patsy now, not after our little high-temperature interlude. Whether or not they heard you say it, they'll assume that you know what I am, as you do. They'll probably think you know what I'm doing, even though you don't. They may even think you're an agent yourself, sent out to help me, maybe somebody I've worked with before."

"Worked?" Isobel smiled. "One day you'll have to tell me all about your work, Mr. Helm. Some of the details sound fascinating."

I said, "Tell you, hell. The way you've fixed it, Mrs. Marner, you stand a good chance of learning all about it firsthand. I think we can safely say that you are now involved in it up to your pretty neck."

She was silent for a moment. Then she reached out and covered my hand with hers. "Maybe that's what I really wanted, Matt. Maybe I like being involved. It's certainly a lot more amusing than sitting in Honolulu watching fat Mainland tourists dress up like fat Hawaiian natives."

I moved my shoulders slightly. "As I've said before,

how you get your kicks is your business. I just hope your sense of humor bears up under the strain."

Isobel laughed and patted my hand lightly and took her hand away. I leaned back, regarding her across the table. Our mild argument had no real significance, because for the moment we had that kind of special understanding that comes between two people who have just learned certain things about each other in the only way those things can be learned. I don't mean that we now liked each other better or trusted each other more than we had before; this had nothing to do with the emotions or the intellect. It was strictly a physical thing and probably quite temporary, but it was kind of comfortable while it lasted.

She looked, however, remarkably unlike a lady who'd just been making passionate physical discoveries in bed. Her dark hair was quite smooth again, and her subdued lipstick was beautifully applied. There was no unbecoming shine to her nose or betraying flush to her cheeks. The inevitable California sunglasses gave her a remote and mysterious look.

She was wearing a slim, short, sleeveless cocktail dress in a silk print of large stylized flowers, predominantly red, on a white background. Somehow, despite the bold design, it managed to look neither gaudy nor native, just summery and elegant. The dress made no great point of baring a lot of back and shoulder; in fact, it was quite discreet in those areas, but it was draped quite low in front. In this modern age of athletic, sunbaked babes, I discovered, an old-fashioned snow-white bosom has a kind of tender appeal.

Isobel smiled faintly when she saw where I was looking, but she made no phony-modest gesture of rearranging her bodice; the view was there to be admired. She was quite a girl. Her green glasses reflected the architectural patterns of the hotel behind me, in a distorted way. I reached out, on a hunch, and drew them off gently and looked through them, and laughed.

"What's so funny?" she asked, rather defensively.

"You wouldn't understand," I said. "It's a kind of

reverse twist. I once met a girl who was pretending to be somebody else, somebody who wore glasses. Only this girl's eyesight was perfectly good, so she just had windowpanes in her goggles. Now you come along with what look like ordinary sunglasses, and they turn out to have prescription lenses."

"Of course," Isobel said. She laughed. "Isn't a woman allowed a little vanity? I can't wear contact lenses, my eyes get all bloodshot and bulgy-looking. And ordinary, clear spectacles make any girl look like a frumpy schoolmarm. But dark glasses make her look like a movie star in disguise. I hope."

"Well, stick with them," I said. "They may come in handy; you never know. There are times when a bit of broken glass can be very useful."

She made a face. "Don't go getting any melodramatic ideas about my fifty-dollar specs," she said. "Besides, I'm half-blind without them. What happened to the girl?"

"What girl?"

"The one who was pretending to be somebody else."

"She died," I said.

"Oh." After a moment, Isobel said quietly. "I won't ask how it happened. I don't think I want to know. Besides, you wouldn't tell me."

"You don't and I wouldn't," I agreed. "If you're finished with that drink, we might try eating for a change. . . . Wait a minute. Let's get things settled first." I studied her thoughtfully. "How seasick do you get in small boats at night?"

Her gray eyes widened a bit at the abrupt question. "I've never been seasick in my life, Matt."

"Well, there's always a first time," I said. "There's a supposedly deserted coastline I want to take a look at without anybody knowing. Way over there on Molokai. . . . No, don't turn your head."

"I'm sorry. That was silly of me. Are we being watched?"

I didn't answer her question. I said, "It'll be a long, wet boat ride against the wind, even if I manage to promote some kind of reasonably reliable craft back in

Lahaina. That's where I was going this evening to make the arrangements, while you were nursing your headache in bed. I was more or less planning to take off immediately if things looked right. However, now that you've revealed yourself as my willing accomplice, I don't dare leave you behind. Once I disappear, they'll want to know exactly what I'm up to, and if you're still around, they'll most likely come to you for the answer. That could get pretty rough. So you're probably safer out there with the wind and the spray in your hair."

She said calmly, "When it comes to boats, I'm not exactly Lady Columbus, but I have done a bit of sailing from time to time. When do we leave?"

"Easy, easy," I said, grinning. "You're such an impulsive dame. We're going in to dinner now, but halfway through I'll have to pay a visit to the men's room. I won't come back. You'll tap your foot impatiently, finish your dessert, smoke an indignant cigarette, and come back out here. You'll sit here, drowning your sorrows in a ladylike way. That'll keep our hatchet-faced friend busy here, watching you. He's up on that side terrace now with his little binoculars. Don't look. Let him think he's invisible."

"I wasn't looking."

"That'll give me only one guy to cope with, I hope. Kamehameha Junior, who's probably hanging around the car. I'll get him out of the way somehow, between here and Lahaina, and make arrangements for the boat. By the time I get back to you here, you'll have worked up a real good mad at me. We'll go off into the dark to quarrel privately—and see if we can't suck in our snooping friend up there and put him out of action, too. Temporarily, of course. Fortunately, I've got lots of sleepy-juice for my little hypo. Then we'll grab some seaworthy clothing from our rooms and take off. Okay?"

"It's . . . very clever," she said, watching me steadily. "Do you know what it sounds like, Matt?"

"What?"

She spoke without expression. "It sounds just like the kind of story a man would tell a girl he was planning to ditch, to keep her quiet until he was safely on his way. How do I know you'll be back?"

I laughed, and picked up the dark glasses, and reached across the table to set them carefully on her nose. "You don't." I said. "But while you're waiting to find out, don't drink too much. There's nothing worse than a hangover at sea."

Three quarters of an hour later, with most of a good steak inside me, I made my excuses and left the table. The dark-faced man had come in while we ate; he was having his dinner alone at a table for two near the door. I walked past him without looking at him. Outside the dining room, I turned toward the john, but I didn't go in. Instead I made a circle around the fancy fountain in the center of the lobby. There was a lot of tropical greenery spotted around in pots and planters. I stopped behind something exotic with big shiny leaves. From there I could see straight through the wide dining room doors to where Isobel was sitting.

She didn't keep me waiting very long. She didn't do any of the stalling I'd suggested; she didn't even have dessert and coffee. She just finished what was on her plate, got the waiter, signed the check, and came toward me, opening her purse. She took out a cigarette, hesitated, and stopped at the hatchet-faced man's table.

He looked up and rose politely to supply a match. I saw her lips move, whispering, as she bent toward the flame. Then she thanked him with a reserved little smile, came out, and crossed the lobby and went out of sight, a slender, lovely, smartly dressed woman with, you'd have thought, nothing on her mind except possibly the impression she was making on the other fashionable tourists in this classy place.

I sighed. It was too bad. She'd put on a great act. Her sister-in-law story had been a stroke of genius, and I still didn't know just how much of it, if any, had been the truth. But she'd overplayed her part in the end. They very often do, the women in our line of work. They have this oddball theory that sex has got something to do with business, and that the way to make sure of a man and allay his suspicions is to seduce him at the earliest possible moment.

Unfortunately, I've never quite managed to convince myself that I'm so fascinating that every girl in the world just naturally wants to drag me into bed. When it does happen, as today, I automatically ask myself what the lady could be after besides love. Well, it looked as if I was on the way to finding out. . . .

Chapter Sixteen

I CONFIRMED, OF COURSE. A lighted cigarette and a few whispered words could hint of treachery, but they weren't proof. You might be able to think up an innocent explanation if you thought hard enough, and jumping to unfavorable conclusions about people is an occupational hazard in a trade like ours, full of disillusioned characters with a low opinion of human nature. I'd had some embarrassing experiences along those lines myself. So I confirmed.

I tailed the man cautiously when he came out of the dining room some ten minutes later, having checked his watch several times in the interim, as if he were anxious not to be late for an important engagement. He led me around the hotel a bit as a matter of routine and pulled one or two of the standard see-behind-you tricks, but he didn't really expect to catch anybody following him, so he didn't. She must have convinced him I was safely on my way to Lahaina. Quite soon he gave up being careful and headed down a path toward the beach. She was waiting for him in the shadows.

They talked for quite a while down there. I didn't risk trying to sneak in close enough to overhear the conversation. The fact that it was taking place was enough. It was beginning to look very much as if my first hunch in Honolulu had been correct, despite Monk's denials, and the woman had been planted on me very cleverly with a most convincing cover story. In any case, whoever she was she could hardly have a motive for conferring secretly with one of Monk's men that meant anything but trouble for me.

They parted company at last, and he walked down toward the shore, while she came up the path to the hotel. She passed quite close to where I crouched in the bushes. I watched her out of sight, noting that, unlike the average woman in a narrow dress and high heels, she managed to walk without excessive posterior undulations. She looked respectable and restrained and expensive, obviously a very high type of lady, the kind who'd never dream of giving herself to a man casually, merely to win his confidence.

I made a face at my thoughts and told myself that everything was fine. Just great. This new development had actually improved my situation. Trustworthy women are a menace to have around, I told myself, particularly when they're beautiful as well. You get to feeling responsible for them and their damn beauty. Tricky, double-crossing females, on the other hand, regardless of looks, make no demands on the conscience, and they can be very useful. For instance, they often know things the trustworthy ladies don't.

I slipped out of my hiding place and headed for the car, telling myself that I was really a very smart fellow and they should have known better than to try to put one over on Matthew Helm. So I got into the car and somebody rose from the floor behind—where I should have looked but hadn't—and stuck a gun in my ear. That's approximately what happens in this racket whenever you start thinking about how very smart you are.

"Take it easy, Eric," said a youthful male voice I recognized. "This is Francis. Bill Menander, remember? It's your turn to keep looking straight ahead or comes it a big hole in the head. You'd better check your dose, Mr. Helm. I only slept for an hour and fifteen minutes on what you gave me back there at the porpoise farm."

I said, "I'll tell the lab. What happens now?"

"You pass your gun back here, very slowly."

"Here it comes." I held it up and felt it taken away. "And now?"

Before he could answer, somebody came running up to the car. "Okay, Bill," said a breathless man's voice that I didn't recognize. "I got the *kanaka*. He's out cold."

"For how long?"

"For long enough. Let's get out of here before Pressman comes looking for his tough beach boy. . . . Move over, you!"

I moved over. There were, of course, all kinds of spectacular responses I could have made, but most of them are designed to leave people dead on the ground. Taking a gun away from a man is risky business at best. Taking it away from him without hurting him isn't something you want to try unless you've got a life or two to spare. And there were some interesting angles here. It seemed better to explore them cautiously than to act like a hero agent with a short fuse.

I sat docilely in the right front seat, therefore, with the gun at my neck, while the unknown youth beside me drove us down the hotel hill and south along the coast highway.

"What's a *kanaka*?" I asked at last.

The driver glanced at me irritably, as if to tell me to shut up, but Francis answered behind me, "It used to mean just a man. Well, a native man. I think Jack London once wrote a story called 'The Kanaka Surf.' That was the big he-man surf that only natives could handle, as opposed to the *malahini* surf, the little surf suitable for tourists to play in. It used to be a proud word, I guess, but people took to using it in a derogatory way, so now . . . Well, you've got to be kind of careful whom you call a *kanaka*. It's kind of like calling a Mexican a greaser. I mean, Rog here wouldn't call Mister Glory a *kanaka* to his face, would you, Rog."

The driver said, "Go to hell. I'm not scared of that beach bum. You should have seen the way I took care of him. He never knew what hit him."

"Mister Glory?" I said. "Who's that, the bronze character in the jeep?"

"His real name is Jimmy Hanohano," Francis said. "He's supposed to be descended from kings or something."

The youth called Rog said, "So what? So's every Mick I ever met."

Francis said, "Anyway, Hanohano means honor or glory in Hawaiian, so he called himself Mister Glory in a band he had for a while. Mister Glory and his Surf Kings. He still sings and plays in the bars—that Beyond-the-Reef kind of mush—and makes love to the female *malahinis*. They really go for him. He can do the old-time slack-string guitar bit, too, real ethnic, but you've got to catch him in the mood. But you don't want to meet him drunk with a broken bottle in his hand."

"Ah, shut up," said Rog. "You sound like his press agent or something. He's not so damn tough."

"Well, I just hope you laid him out good. He's one guy I don't want any trouble with. And Pressman's another. That hatchet-faced creep would order us killed like ordering eggs for breakfast."

"Maybe he already has. Or the Monk has. *There's* the only guy who scares me. Those damn blue eyes of his. . . . Hang on, we might as well turn here and get off the road a bit."

As we swerved, the headlights flashed across one of the colorful tourist-bureau markers put up to identify local points of interest. Then we were bouncing along a dirt track through the big Hawaiian mesquites—excuse me, *kiawes*. The road emerged from the trees and dove into a sugarcane field that seemed endless in the dark: just interminable rows of tall green cane sliding into the lights on either side of the car. Finally this gave way to a canyon of sorts, heading up into the invisible hills. Rog stopped the car under a wall of rock and cut the lights and the ignition. There was a little silence after the engine had died. Francis tapped me on the shoulder.

"Here's your gun, Mr. Helm," he said, holding it out to me butt first.

I looked at it, a little startled. As I say, we're disillusioned and suspicious; we don't believe in Santa Claus
at all. And there are a number of nasty routines that
start with giving the prisoner back his gun. Before I
could make up my mind to grasp the weapon, Rog had
reached out and snatched it from Francis' hand.

"Have you lost your everlasting marbles?"

Francis said, "We need the man's help, don't we? He's
the only guy we can turn to. So who's going to help
looking down a gun barrel, yet? Give it back to him." He
spoke to me: "Sorry about the holdup, sir, but we had to
talk to you and you were being watched. There wasn't
any quick way to explain without letting the whole world
know. . . . Give it back to him, Rog!"

"Take it easy. Let's hear what he can do for us before
we get so damn generous with the firearms. Ask him
about Jill."

"What about Jill?" I demanded.

"That's what we want to know, Mr. Helm," Francis
said. "She told us she had a kind of date with you this
morning. We know she was trying to make up her mind
about telling you . . . " He stopped.

"Telling me what?"

Rog asked suspiciously, "Did you see her this morning?"

"Yes, I saw her. She checked me out on a surfboard.
Well, more or less."

Rog said sourly, "That must have been something
to see!"

I regarded him for a moment. There was enough light
to make him out after a fashion: one of those handsome,
tanned, sneering, dime-a-dozen boys with streaky, too-
long hair. Not that I have any objection to long haircuts.
Wild Bill Hickock wore his to the shoulders and nobody
was heard to complain. But then, Hickock had a little
more than hair going for him. All you could say for Rog
was that he was making his associate, Francis, look
better all the time, despite the plump face and the silly
little moustache.

Francis said, "Lay off, Rog. Don't mind him, Mr.

Helm. He's just scared. We're both scared. We don't know what the hell we've got ourselves into, sir, and now the Kilauea Street house is closed and nobody answers the phone and Lanny's dead and Jill's disappeared. You don't know where she is? She claimed you'd been sent to investigate the information she'd passed to Washington. She was going to identify herself to you as soon as she dared. Didn't she tell you anything while you were out there together this morning?"

I didn't answer at once. The fact that Jill had apparently confided freely in these boys was a blow; it made a joke of our attempts at security—particularly now that Francis had blabbed the essential facts to the warm night air. It wasn't hard to decide how far I trusted him and his associate; I didn't trust them at all. Even if they were sincere, which hadn't been proved, they were obviously inexperienced and not too bright in professional matters.

However, this wasn't really important now because there was somebody out in the dark whom I trusted even less, somebody who'd already heard too much.

Chapter Seventeen

I DIDN'T KNOW WHO was out there, of course. My hearing and experience simply told me we were being stalked, like moose in a meadow. Just guessing, I eliminated Isobel. It didn't seem like her kind of assignment; certainly she hadn't been dressed for it when last seen. I figured it was probably either the hawk-faced man I now had a name for, Pressman, or his boy Hanohano, known as Mister Glory. Rog claimed to have put the latter to sleep for a reasonable period, but Rog wasn't a source I considered completely reliable.

In any case, discretion was useless now. We'd been talking in normal tones and the car windows were open. It was a quiet night up here in the foothills, good for eavesdropping. I had to assume that the man out in the dark had heard facts about Jill he could not be allowed to repeat. A few more wouldn't hurt. He might as well get a good earful while I tolled him in to where he could be silenced.

I said, speaking loudly and clearly, "Well, as a matter of fact she did tell me a few things. But she didn't tell me she'd taken all of Hawaii into her confidence. I thought the girl was being careful, for God's sake! Who else knows that she's been in contact with Washington?"

"Just us, Mr. Helm," Francis said. "And Lanny, but he's dead."

"Who's Lanny and how's he dead?"

"There were four of us—Jill, Lanny, Rog, and me. We . . . we kind of worked together. You know, on the peace bit. Jill was the spark plug, she was full of ideas. . . ."

"Sure. She gave me that weep-for-the-toiling-Asian-masses line. Never mind that. Get to Lanny, who's dead where?"

Francis said with a hint of stubbornness, "Well, first you'd better know how we all got recruited, sir. You see, after one of our meetings, Jill met this man who called himself Rath—"

"Monk," I said. "She told me. He sold her the idea and she sold you. You were all going to save the world for peace on government pay."

The stalker was moving in closer. I couldn't really believe the boys hadn't heard him, but city kids—kids who've never spent time in the woods with a rabbit gun or deer rifle—are practically deaf. Or perhaps they knew perfectly well he was out there. Perhaps this was a setup and their job was to make me talk for the man out in the dark, whoever he might be. For the moment I was happy to oblige.

Rog said angrily, "Hell, man, it's our lives they want to throw away out in those crummy jungles. A man's got a right to say what he's going to get killed for, hasn't he?"

I saw no need to get involved in that argument. I just asked, "What did Lanny get killed for? Or did he die a natural death?"

"He died of a broken neck," Francis said, and shivered. "I think Monk did that, personally. Lanny's lying there in the house on Kilauea Street with his head all twisted to one side. . . . Mr. Helm, I think we were played for suckers. I think Monk, for some reason, wanted a bunch of young people with pacifist records, wanted them on the rolls, so to speak, to cover what he was really doing with the men whose names never showed on the books. I mean, we never got any real training, not to amount to anything. And nobody got reprimanded for getting involved in political affairs—or staying involved. You'd almost have thought Monk liked having us attract attention. And we never had much to do. Shadowing you was the first real assignment I was given. I guess I was pretty clumsy at it."

"Let's just say I spotted you," I said. "I thought I was supposed to. Now, if you don't mind, let's bear down on your friend Lanny. He's dead with a broken neck in the house on Kilauea Street. That's the house in Honolulu Monk was using as headquarters?"

"Officially," Francis said. "I'm beginning to think that was kind of a front, too."

"Now the house is shut up? Nobody's there except Lanny, dead?"

"That's right," Rog said. "Jeez, we practically fell over him when we broke in."

Francis said, "You see, Mr. Helm, we tried to call, to report in and ask for instructions, and we got no answer at any of the usual numbers. I mean, I tried after I woke up—you'd given me a message to deliver, remember—and then I got hold of Rog, and I tried to reach Lanny and Jill, but I couldn't. We tried the contact numbers again. No soap. So we drove on out there and the place was empty. No cars, nobody answering the door, nothing. Except Lanny's Honda. We walked around and found a window half open and crawled in and found him. Lanny, I mean. I figure he did like we did, tried to call, and then drove out when he got no answer. But when he got there somebody was still there, and Lanny saw something he shouldn't have, so he got killed."

"What about Jill?" I asked. "You couldn't locate her anywhere?"

"No."

Rog said, "You haven't told him about the boat."

"We checked on the boat, after leaving the house," Francis said. "The smaller boat, the one with the twin Evinrude seventies. It's missing. The other, the big inboard-outboard job, has been gone for a couple of days."

"So Jill told me," I said.

"That's what you say," Rog said. "It seems to me we're telling you a lot of stuff and you're not telling us a damn thing. Just what did you and Jill talk about, out there in the surf? If you did talk."

The stalker was quite close now. Because of the cliff near which we were parked, he was making his approach from the left side, which was fine with me. It put Rog more or less between him and me. I hoped the boy was reasonably bullet-proof, if it came to that. I couldn't think of a better use for him.

I said, "Just a couple more questions before I tell you. First, did you ever hear of a place called K?" They shook their heads. I went on, "And Lanny was just dead? That's all? Nothing fancy, no cigarette burns or anything to indicate he'd been made to talk?"

"No, sir," Francis said. "Nothing like that."

"Then we can hope that Jill is still in the clear. Assuming she's alive, of course. I mean, neither of you has spilled any of this to anybody else?"

Rog said, "What do you think we are, stupid? Hell, if Monk knew we'd got together and arranged to have her contact Washington, he'd kill us all!"

"And what made you decide to contact Washington?"

"I told you, sir," Francis said. "It began to look as if he was playing us for suckers. As if he had something big on—big and dangerous and, well, treasonable—and we'd be left holding the bag. When Jill said he'd been in touch with Peking—"

Rog said, "So I think the draft stinks and the war is for the birds, but it's all in the family, if you know what

I mean. If Monk wants to ring in a bunch of Chinks, he can play without me. I'm cutting out. Now, what arrangements did you make with Jill?"

"I'll tell you," I said, and lowered my voice to a confidential whisper, and started telling them. I used the truth. It was easier than thinking up a lie and made no difference at this point.

It worked like a charm. I mean, with my voice down he could no longer hear me out there, so he started to move in even closer to improve the reception, but good as he was he wasn't quite good enough for that. The boys might be deaf, but they weren't that deaf. Suddenly Francis held up a hand for silence, and I stopped talking, and Rog reached out abruptly and hit the lights, and there he was, almost on top of us, the golden boy himself, with a shiny revolver in his hand.

He threw himself to the side, and fired. It was great shooting, for a man half-blinded by headlights. I heard Rog take the first bullet; I didn't wait to find out where the second was going. I just fell out the door and ran like hell. There was more gunfire behind me as I ran. I heard one shot that had a dull, muffled sound, fired from inside the car. Hanohano's answering two shots echoed sharp and clear between the walls of the canyon.

Then I was at the bend where the road turned into the sugarcane field. There was one final, sharp report behind me, and a bullet struck the dirt somewhere to the left and ricocheted on past me nastily. I turned the corner out of sight, unhit, leaving Mister Glory, I figured, with just one live round in his weapon if it was our usual five-shot model—two, if it was a six-shooter. It didn't really matter. If he knew his stuff at all, and I thought he did, he wouldn't come charging blindly after me with an almost-empty gun. He'd pause to reload, and to listen, and to make plans.

I gave him something to listen to, therefore. I kept pounding noisily along the road through the cane field, like a scared man intent on nothing but flight. As I ran I caught a glimpse of a vehicle backed into a track leading off to the left: the topless jeep. I continued past this, gradually slowing down, as if I were running out of strength and wind, which wasn't far from the truth. Finally I was down to a breathless, almost soundless shuffle. Hanohano had heard, I hoped, a convincing pattern of receding footsteps gradually dying away as the runner's distance and his weariness increased.

I turned and, moving as silently as I could manage, stole quickly back to the jeep. It was still standing in the cane, its glass and metal gleaming dully. I took a chance and went right up to it, gambling that I had beat the owner to it. I won my gamble. Nobody jumped me or shot at me. I stood there a moment, listening. There was no sound but a general rustling as breezes moved through the field around me. I picked my spot as carefully as if I'd been selecting a stand beside a game trail, and stepped back into the cane, and got some equipment ready to receive Mister Glory.

I was still gambling, of course. He might have outsmarted me by simply heading off across country to the nearest phone, on foot. From there he could have called his radio contact—I presumed he had one—and got word to K, wherever it was, letting Monk know there was a female traitor inside the gates, if she'd actually made it there.

With important information to be transmitted, that would have been the safe and conservative thing for Hanohano to do. There was nothing I had that he needed, and the jeep would keep. But he was tough, I reminded myself, and it was his jeep, and he wasn't likely to walk when he could ride. He was a descendant of Hawaiian kings, and he wouldn't make detours around any damn *haoles*—white men to you. At least I was betting that was how his mind would work.

Again I won my bet; he came. He came quite silently this time. I've done a bit of stalking myself, but I'm willing to admit you can generally hear me coming if you know I'm on the way and listen hard. This one moved like a ghost. He must have been hurried or careless or overconfident up the canyon. Perhaps he'd wanted to get into position fast so he could overhear as much as possible; perhaps he'd just figured we'd be too busy talking to notice. But now he knew that if I was here at all, I was ready and laying for him, and he gave me no warning at all of his approach.

Suddenly he was just there with the shiny revolver in his hands, slipping through the scattered canes at the edge of the road. Every few steps he'd stop to listen. Well, I can't move that noiselessly, but I'm a real expert at holding still. I've had lots of practice, in everything from a duck blind to a fifty-man ambush. I just crouched there and waited him out and let him come to me. When he was within reach, I swung the belt.

He was almost too quick for me. I missed wrapping the leather around the wrist as I'd intended. But the heavy buckle smashed across his hand and sent the gun flying. He dove for it, but he had to hit short and flat to avoid being scalped by my second swing. He gave up the gun and came to his feet like a cat, facing me.

He had no shirt on. He'd shed that, perhaps because it was too gaudy or too noisy, or just because he functioned better with a minimum of clothing. He'd also shed his shoes, which seemed to be a habit of the Islands—I remembered the barefoot hula dancer in the elaborate brocade gown. The vague light from the sky gleamed on his powerful chest and shoulders. His hands and forearms swung threateningly, clublike, hinting at karate. I certainly couldn't match strength with him, and probably not skill, either. Well, I had no idea of trying. This wasn't a friendly match in the neighborhood gym. The man had to die before he could tell what he had heard.

"Don't use that belt on me, man," he whispered. "Don't you use it, I say. I'll tear you apart if you do."

I laughed. "Hanohano, you're a fraud. If I had the time, I'd beat hell out of you. As it is, I'll be nice. I'll merely kill you."

His white teeth flashed in the darkness as he grinned. "So now we've both pounded our chests like monkeys. So now let's fight. Coming at you, *haole*!"

He crouched, feinted, and sprang at me, and I side-stepped and whipped the belt across and almost got him.

He had to drop and roll to escape the singing buckle. He was up again in an instant, coming in again with that clumsy-looking, weaving gait. I backed away slowly, holding the belt before me, swinging it from side to side until I saw that it held his eyes—until I saw that he had the idea I was trying to give him. Then I stepped forward and swung, giving him a long, looping teaser this time.

It was slow and easy. He had all day to grab it, and he did. He pulled hard, and I went in ahead of his pull. Braced, he was thrown off balance when he met no resistance. We came together and went down, and as we fell, I brought my little knife from behind my back and put it into him to the hilt, left-handed. I took time to strike once more, higher and more accurately, and rolled free and kept rolling. A knife hasn't got the shocking power of a bullet. A man can be dead from a knife wound and still have plenty of time to kill you before the message reaches his brain: *you're dead.*

I found my feet and looked for him, ready to dodge, or run, or step in and finish him, whichever seemed more appropriate. But he hadn't got further than his knees. He was kneeling there by the jeep, covering his wounds with his big brown hands, looking up at me accusingly while the blood oozed between his fingers. I moved in closer to him, but not very close. There wasn't any sense in taking further risks this late in the game.

He licked his lips. "You . . . you tricked me, *haole!*"

It was no time to apologize. He didn't want my apologies. He wanted to know that he was dying at the hands of a man, not of a kid who would weep over his kills.

I said harshly, "I'm a pro, *kanaka*. I don't fight for pleasure, just for keeps."

He showed me his big, bright grin again. "Too bad for you, man. You'll miss a lot of fun that way. A lot of fun. . . ."

Then the message got through to the brain at last, and his face changed, and he pitched forward in the dirt of the cane field. I waited a little while, as you do, and checked the pulse cautiously, and couldn't find it. He wasn't playing possum. He was dead. And the funny thing was, I'd never known him, but I was going to miss him anyway.

I rose, assuring myself that the important thing was that Jill's secret was safe—at least it would not be betrayed by the man at my feet. For the moment I had trouble convincing myself that any secret was that important. I got into the jeep. The key was in the ignition. I started the battered vehicle, switched on the lights, and drove around the dead man on the ground and back up the canyon to where my rented Ford was parked. Mister Glory had done a good job there. Rog was dead with a bullet in the head. Francis, with two in the chest, was going fast.

"You . . . you left us!" he whispered when I opened the car door and bent over him. It seemed I wasn't living up to anybody's idea of proper behavior tonight. "You ran away!"

"You boys had all the guns," I said. "What was I supposed to do, just sit there and throw rocks at the guy?"

"Where is he? Hanohano?"

"He won't be back," I said.

"Did you . . . did you get him?"

"I got him."

"Ah . . ." Francis was silent for a little, breathing painfully. "There's something . . . That woman. McLain."

For a moment, the name rang no bells. I'd already got used to thinking of her as Marner, which probably wasn't her real name, either.

"What about Isobel McLain?"

"That search of her room . . . just a phony to make you think. . . . Watch out for . . . watch out. . . ." He stopped. I thought he was gone, but then he whispered, "Jill. Good kid. The only one of us left. . . . Save. . . ."

"I'll save her," I said.

It was a promise I might find difficult to keep, but it didn't matter. He was dead. Everybody was dead on Maui tonight. Everybody but me.

Chapter Eighteen

AT LEAST THAT WAS the way it seemed out there in the foothills. When I got to Lahaina, I discovered that there were actually quite a few people still alive on the island; in fact, the streets were full of them. At the edge of town I got off the main thoroughfare to park the jeep, figuring that it was probably known and might attract attention, driven by a stranger. At that, it was better than the rental sedan, full of blood and bullet holes. Besides, it had a plain old foot-powered brake and a real gearbox, the kind you stirred with a big stick. I could drive it fine.

I walked into town and found a phone booth down by the dock and stood inside watching the colorful, sunburned people, local and transient, circulating through the joint on the corner, a frame hotel, restaurant, and bar that seemed to be a relic of the old whaling days when the whole Pacific came to this port to get liquored and laid. I was waiting for an overseas connection. Normally I'd have called our Honolulu relay and he'd have put me straight through, but I had to assume that the whole Hawaii apparatus was in Monk's hands, so I was calling direct. It took a while before I heard the voice of the girl in Washington. Then Mac came on.

"Eric here," I said. "Uncover."

This meant that I was through playing games and we didn't have to waste time pretending to be what we weren't.

"Very well, Eric. Proceed."

"The background first, sir."

I gave it to him fast, everything that had happened to date. As I talked, I watched a piratical character in dirty white pants and a striped jersey who'd come wandering out on the veranda of the old hotel and seemed to be very carefully not looking in my direction. All he needed was a wooden leg and a patch over one eye.

"There you have it, sir," I finished. "If you really want to keep all this quiet, as you once intimated, you'd better get a cleanup squad here from somewhere before daybreak. Let's hope nobody uses that road for a lover's lane tonight. Tell them to turn at the tourist-bureau sign pointing to some petroglyphs up the canyon. The Olowalu Petroglyphs. In case you're wondering, a petroglyph is an inscription or picture story carved on rock. We've got some good ones back home in New Mexico."

"Indeed? I wasn't really wondering, Eric. Proceed."

"Yes, sir. They should have no trouble finding the car and its contents where I told you. The other body is back down the road about two hundred yards and off to the south in the cane about thirty yards. The jeep tracks will lead them there. Tell them to look around for Hanohano's gun; I didn't take time to find it. Incidentally, how does it happen these Pacific people are getting the new stainless steel model while we've got to make do with the old blue job that rusts on sight?"

Mac said, "At the rate you reportedly go through guns, Eric, they don't have time to rust, so what difference does it make? Hold on while I get some people moving."

Waiting, I glanced toward the veranda, but the pirate in the striped jersey had disappeared. Some pretty girls in muu-muus were talking to some handsome young men in the long, baggy swim trunks that seem to be fashionable nowadays, a change from the glorified jockstraps of a few years back. The men reminded me of Rog, which was nothing in their favor.

"They'll be on Maui by midnight," Mac's voice said in my ear. I made note of the fact that he must have had some trustworthy people standing by somewhere in the Islands, or he could not have hoped to get them here so soon. He confirmed this by saying, "What is your plan, Eric? Will you need help?"

I said, "The only help I'll need, where I'm going, is already there—or it isn't. As for my plan, it's essentially the old Trojan Horse routine: get yourself hauled inside the enemy citadel somehow and hope for the best. If Jill has made it, it should work out, with a little luck. If she hasn't. . . ."

"Precisely," Mac said. "You are gambling three times, Eric. You are gambling that this place, K, is actually on Molokai. Also, you are gambling, I gather, that if you get yourself captured near enough to it, you will be taken inside alive instead of simply being killed—"

I said, "Of course, if I can locate the hideout without being spotted and slip into it unseen, I'll do it. But those are two big ifs."

Mac went on as if I hadn't spoken, "And finally you are gambling that if you are brought into the place, the girl will be there and in a position to help you."

"My luck's been running pretty good so far tonight, sir," I said. "I'm just going to have to take the chance that Jill gave me the right general location and that Monk will react to my presence the way I expect. I mean, he's hated me for a long time, sir. And you can't gloat over a dead enemy like you can over a live one. It isn't nearly as much fun."

"Very well, but you are dealing with a man who's acquainted with all our techniques and equipment, a man who's even been on assignment with you and knows the way you work. As his prisoner, you aren't likely to outwit him without help. If the girl is not there, or if she fails you—" He was silent for a little. "Perhaps it would be better if you leave her to do what she can there, while you try to pinpoint the location cautiously, after which you call up reinforcements."

"How? I mean, hell, we could call in the whole U.S. Navy and have them search all the Islands, and do you think Monk hasn't thought of that? They'd eventually find where he'd been, but they'd never find him. One man he'll maybe let come in close, particularly if that man is yours truly. He knows you almost invariably work me more or less alone. And he's got a score to pay, or thinks he has. But the minute signals start flying and it begins to look like a group operation he'll be long gone. And what could you tell the Navy anyway, sir? That one of our men has been acting a bit funny, and we think he's up to something kind of big, but we don't know what it is? But we'd like to have them turn out the Fleet and muster the Marines just the same. Hell, they'd laugh in your face, sir. Besides, he'll have arranged to be notified of any unusual naval activity, you can bet on that."

"The Navy was not my suggestion, Eric. Of course, I have considered it, but as you say, persuading them to take appropriate action under adequate security would be very difficult since we really don't know what we're up against." He paused. "You still have no idea what Monk's intentions are?"

"No, sir. He seems to be going in all directions at once. On the one hand, we've got his tame peace-in-Asia front; and on the other, we have the two mysterious specialists from Peking with whatever they brought in their luggage. I can't imagine what technical project it could be that would have Monk asking help of a bunch of Chinese. Explosives of some kind would be the logical answer, but he's pretty competent along those lines himself. Of course if it's something real big and nasty and nuclear, he might not have adequate facilities—"

"That's mere guesswork," Mac said. "And I can't see the Chinese, with their limited nuclear capacity, turning any material of that nature over to an American agent, even a turncoat one."

"I hope you're right," I said. "But what it amounts to is that we simply don't know which way he's going to jump. We just know he'll jump soon. After all, he shut up the Honolulu place with a dead man on the floor, and he knows as well as anybody that there's a limit to how long a body can lie around without getting itself discovered. Incidentally, I should have had you tell the boys to take care of that one, too, when they get a chance."

"I did tell them," Mac said.

"Yes, sir," I said. "We can assume, therefore, that

Monk intends to act within, say, the next forty-eight hours. Are you still in official contact?"

"The routine Pacific reports are still coming through on schedule."

"Sure. He wouldn't alert you by cutting them off. But I bet you can't reach him personally."

"I haven't tried. It seemed best to leave him alone." Mac hesitated. "You are counting heavily on this girl, Eric. You realize that, of course."

"No, sir," I said. "On the contrary, I am counting on her very lightly. That's just the point."

"What do you mean?"

I said, "Hell, I don't like to stick my neck out any better than the next man. If I knew for sure she'd got there, and if I thought she could handle it alone, I'd be strongly tempted to leave her to it. Putting myself in Monk's hands isn't something I really look forward to, sir. But the fact is, our Jill is a fairly weak reed. In spite of my final instructions, I'm willing to bet she won't do the job without me, even if it's right there to be done and she's right there to do it. She's a nice girl, and her intentions are swell, and she looks like a brave young goddess, but there's something strangely lacking in the fortitude department, if you know what I mean. Look at the way she tried to pin you down with that no-risk agreement. Look at the way I had to shame her into cooperating at all. She's just a college kid playing secret agent; she won't act without somebody right there to hold her hand. Even then, all I'm really hoping for is that she'll have guts enough to bring a knife when the time comes to cut the ropes."

"I see." Mac was silent, thousands of miles away. I could visualize him frowning. "That makes the odds still heavier against you."

I said, "However, there's one factor I neglected to mention."

"What's that?"

"I promised her I'd come if I could possibly make it." He made some kind of sound. It sounded like a snort. Apparently he thought no more of my promises to Jill than he did of his own. Well, honor isn't taken very seriously in our line of work. I said, "Yes, sir. I will give your regards to the Monk, sir, if the opportunity arises. Eric, signing off."

Leaving the booth, I saw my skulking pirate lounging in the doorway of the saloon. He resolutely paid no attention to me as I went into the place and got the barman to steer me to a young fellow who, for a fairly substantial consideration, was willing to take a lady and a gentleman for a cozy midnight boat ride. Having made the arrangements, I walked back to the jeep, discreetly shadowed by the gent in the striped jersey, but he made no attempt to get a car and follow me further. Apparently his jurisdiction ended at the Lahaina city limits, and now all he wanted was a phone from which to report to Pressman that I'd run my errands and was on my way home.

I glanced at my watch when I reached the hotel and was surprised at how early it was. Men had died and plans had been laid upon which might depend the fate of nations, but it was only a little past nine o'clock. I looked myself over for dirt or bloodstains that would make me conspicuous inside. I made sure I'd got my belt back through all the loops. I took out my gun. I'd got it back from Rog, who'd never fired it, which was just as well, since it was still loaded with more-or-less blanks.

I'd debated taking Francis' gun, too, but I'd decided that I was better off with just a single gun that could be fixed not to shoot. After all, I still had to deal with the lady who'd caused me to rig it that way in the first place—but first there were some details to take care of. I loaded the weapon with real ammo and went in to take care of them.

Chapter Nineteen

THEY MADE IT very easy for me. Isobel was awaiting me on the cocktail terrace, just as I'd instructed. Pressman was keeping an eye on the situation from the higher side terrace, as before. He seemed to be taking no other precautions. I studied them both from various vantage points in the hotel, to make reasonably sure of this.

Well, there was no need for them to be careful, was there? They knew exactly what I intended to do, didn't they? I mean, I'd given them my plan of action beforehand, and up to this point I'd followed it in every detail, just as I'd told it to Isobel.

I'd driven to Lahaina, getting rid of my shadow on the way, just as I'd said I would. There had been a little more to the journey than that, but the details didn't really matter. And I'd chartered a boat in Lahaina, just as I'd promised Isobel, specifying two passengers, male and female. And now I'd be coming back unsuspectingly to pick up my lady and a change of seagoing clothes and to put Pressman himself out of action just long enough for the two of us to make our nautical getaway.

He wouldn't be looking forward to that, but Isobel would have assured him that I'd specifically mentioned the harmless sleepy-stuff I intended to use on him, so he was probably figuring to go along with the gag. In the meantime, of course, his piratical Lahaina errand boy would be making preparations to pick us up, one way or another, when we arrived at dockside. . . .

It was too bad. Pressman was probably a competent enough guy, just as Hanohano had been a competent enough guy: they just hadn't studied the dossier carefully enough. They kept expecting me to play by some kind of rules, in a game that had no rules. Monk wouldn't have made that mistake, but Monk wasn't here to warn them.

I watched for a little while. There was no great hurry. Besides Pressman's, there was only one table occupied on the higher terrace. Presently the young couple who'd been sitting there rose and left, which was a break for me. Pressman didn't even glance around when I stepped out through the open doors. His man in Lahaina had warned him I was on my way, of course, but he knew where I'd be coming, didn't he?

He was looking for me to appear below, where, alone at a side table, a slender figure in a summery cocktail dress was applying the flame of a lighter to a cigarette with the bored, jerky, angry movements of a neglected woman who is reaching the end of her patience and maybe of her liquor capacity as well.

I said, "Over here, Pressman."

He turned his head quickly, and started to rise, and sank back into his chair. He sat very still, looking at the snub-nosed revolver I held close to my side.

"Eric," he said softly. "What do you want?"

"Your Hawaiian boy was good, Pressman," I murmured. "But he wasn't quite good enough. Would you care to give it a try?"

He was a pro; he just grinned at the challenge. "Hell, no," he said. "Just take it that I'm scared, friend. Guns always scare me. So I'm shaking, see me? Now what do we do?"

"We get up very carefully," I said. "We walk into the hotel. We go to our room—your room. And we keep our hands at our sides in plain sight, because we know that the instant one disappears, we die."

He studied me for a moment, as if trying to guess whether what I had in store for him was still what I'd told Isobel it would be, now that I'd changed the program in other respects. Then he shrugged his narrow shoulders fatalistically and rose. It was a long walk to the room, or so it seemed to me. Maybe it seemed that way to him, too. At the door, he paused to give me a questioning look. I nodded. He reached into his pocket cautiously, produced a key, and unlocked the door. I held him back while I reached inside to turn on the light. Nothing happened. I herded him inside ahead of me and closed the door.

"On the bed," I said. "Face down, if you please."

He hesitated, standing there with his back to me. He wanted, at least, to turn his head once more to look at me before he rendered himself completely helpless. But trying to read minds is for amateurs and mentalists. He was a professional agent.

He moved his shoulders again, and stepped forward, and arranged himself on the bed as instructed. I took three quick steps and pinned him down. I shoved his face into the pillow, slipped the needle into the nape of the neck where the hair would mask the puncture wound, and drove the plunger home.

He knew, then. He knew it was no harmless sleep he was being given, and he made a belated attempt to struggle, but I had him solid and it lasted only a few seconds. Then the stuff reached the brain, or heart, or wherever it goes to do its work.

I drew out the hypo and put it carefully back into my drug kit. I went into the bathroom and got a bit of toilet paper and wiped off the tiny drop of blood that might have called attention to the pinprick on the neck. The stuff itself is almost undetectable, and the symptoms are those of an ordinary coronary, or so I've been told by the guys who cook it up for us. They are very proud of it. Well, we'd soon see if their pride was justified. I went back and flushed the paper down the john, using my handkerchief to turn the handle. Mac's cleanup squad would not be dealing with this one. He had to be found to show I meant business, so it had to look good enough to fool the authorities.

Returning, I looked down at him for a moment. I try to make a point of this. I have no respect for these delicate characters who can commit endless massacres by remote control but can't bear to face their dead at close range. It was a lousy, cold-blooded thing, of course, but I'd had no choice. The harmless drug we carry is good for only four hours at best, and according to Francis, the batch I had now wasn't even up to full strength: he'd claimed to have awakened well ahead of schedule.

I needed more than four hours. Either that, or I needed to look as if I'd done everything humanly and inhumanly possible to buy myself the time, even if I'd failed. If I just walked—or sailed—carelessly into a waiting trap, Monk would guess that I was relying on inside help to save me.

It was tough on Mr. Pressman, but I had to leave enough dead men behind to make it look as if I were trying desperately to cover my tracks. Maybe I was. It depended on how things worked out when I got to K, if I got there.

I picked up my gun, which I had laid aside, and shook out the live rounds I'd loaded out of respect for Pressman. I put the powderless shells back into the chambers. Dealing with a strong man who may be armed is a little different from dealing with a weak—well, relatively weak—woman who probably isn't armed: you shouldn't need a loaded gun to handle her and you don't want to provide her with one to use on you, but you may want to tempt her with a firearm to make her betray herself once and for all. I went to find Isobel.

She was just signing for another drink when I emerged on the cocktail terrace. "Well, it's about time you showed up," she snapped as I sat down beside her. I remembered that I'd told her to pick a fight with me. She went on in convincingly angry tones: "Do you know how long I've been waiting? If you think I came all the way from Honolulu with you just to——"

"Pressman's dead, Duchess," I said softly.

Even the colored glasses couldn't hide the sudden widening of her eyes. I also detected the betraying glance she threw toward the other terrace. She licked her lips. When she spoke, the assumed anger was gone from her voice.

"I . . . I don't know what you're talking about, Matt. Who's dead?"

"Cut it out," I said. "Don't try to fight it. He's dead.

I've just finished killing him. Let's take a little walk
down to the beach and I'll tell you all about it." She
didn't move at once until, standing up again, I made a
sharp little upward gesture with my hand. I reached out
to help her as she rose a bit uncertainly, and I put her
white purse into her hands. "Easy now," I said. "Maybe you'd better cut down on the sauce, Duchess. You
don't look well."

It made her mad enough to pull herself together, as
it was meant to do. She jerked her arm free and threw
me a look that was a mixture of fear and fury. She
moved off the terrace ahead of me, quite steadily now.
I followed her to the head of the shadowed path, and
down through the darkness, and moved up beside her
as she came out on the sand. Again I took her arm to
help her, since she was finding it heavy going in her
high heels. This time she didn't pull away. Instead I
heard her give an odd, sharp, little laugh.

"What's funny?" I asked.

"Those advertisements," she said. "About the glamour
of the tropics. They always show a man and woman in
evening dress strolling along a beach at night. I never
did see anything glamorous about getting sand in my
pumps. Or running around in my stocking feet, either."

"No," I said. "You wouldn't."

She glanced at me suspiciously. After a moment, she
asked, "Are you going to kill me, too, Matt?"

"I'm considering it," I said. "Let's stop here and discuss the matter. You can sit down on that boat if you
like."

She drew her fingertips along the deck to make sure it
was clean and sat down. I sat down beside her. She
made a little ceremony of dumping the sand out of her
shoes. There wasn't much wind down here on the beach,
just an occasional gust. The six little sailboats lay in a
neat row; dark, masted shapes against the light sand.
Up above were the lights of the hotel and of the illumi-
nated terrace from which we had come. It seemed like
another world. I heard Isobel give her sharp, nervous
laugh again.

"I don't think you're really going to kill me, darling," she said. "I don't think you really killed Mr. Pressman. It was . . . it was just a joke, wasn't it?"

"Sure," I said. "I always joke about homicide. Funniest subject on earth. You ought to see him, just for laughs. Lying there on his bed with a blank look on his face and a hypo puncture in the back of his neck. He thought I was just putting him to sleep for a little while. Isn't that a scream? Can you imagine where he got such a ridiculous notion, Duchess?"

She licked her lips again. "Matt, I—"

I went on without letting her finish, "You'd have died laughing when he realized he was actually being killed. Funniest thing I've seen since the power mower threw Uncle Hector and came roaring back to chew him to pieces."

"Matt, please—"

I said, "And then there's Hanohano, if you like good homicidal fun. In case you don't recognize the name, that's the Hawaiian character who followed us from the airport. He's lying out in the sugarcane with two knife holes in his chest. Blood and gore everywhere. Funny, my God! Really a gasser. I'm sorry you missed it; you'd have laughed your head off." I sighed. "Actually, I feel kind of bad about Hanohano. Did you know that the state of Hawaii has a population of nearly three quarters of a million, but there are only about ten thousand native Hawaiians left? They're practically extinct. I feel kind of as if I'd gone out and shot down one of the last trumpeter swans. But if you like jokes, here's the real hilarious thing. When I got to Lahaina after taking care of the Hawaiian, there was a man hanging around the docks. He seemed very interested in me. It was almost as if he'd known I'd be coming. Now, how do you figure he could have learned that? After all, I hadn't told anybody where I was bound. Anybody but you."

She said desperately, "Matt, you don't understand—"

I said in a harsher tone of voice. "You sold me out, Isobel. Or have you been reporting to Monk all along? Anyway, tonight you made love to me, then you got me talking over drinks, and then you betrayed me to the opposition. Now I don't know exactly where you fit into this, or who you really are, or how much you know about this kind of business, but you can't be dumb enough not to know the penalty for being caught the way I've just caught you."

"If you'd let me explain—"

"There's nothing to explain," I said. "I've killed two men tonight, two men against whom I had nothing except that they were in the way. I feel a little bad about that. Not much, but a little. But I wouldn't feel a bit bad about killing you. Native Hawaiians may be in short supply, but the world's never going to run out of double-crossing bitches. Like sparrows and starlings they'll be with us forever. One would never be missed." I paused and went on deliberately, "On the other hand, you may just possibly be of some use to me, Duchess. Not much use, just enough for me to risk leaving you alive for a while *if* you keep your trap shut, *if* you make absolutely no trouble whatsoever, and *if* you do exactly as you're told. No tricks, no arguments. What do you say?"

She licked her lips. "What use do you have for me, Matt? What are you going to do to me?"

"Never mind that. I'll tell you when the time comes."

There was a brief silence. Isobel drew a long breath. "I don't have much choice, do I? All right, I'll do whatever you say, Matt."

I looked at her for a moment, and got to my feet. "Okay. It's a deal. Now you grab this side and I'll grab the other. Let's get it afloat."

She stared at me blankly. "What?"

"The boat, stupid. You didn't really think I was going back to Lahaina, where people are undoubtedly waiting for me—people you sicced on me. Come on, let's put it in the water. Molokai, here we come."

She was on her feet now. "But . . . but you're mad! Why, it's miles and miles of open water! We'd never make it in this little thing!"

I said, "Hell, the Polynesians came clear up from the South Pacific in a hollow log to colonize this place. If

I can't sail a modern, unsinkable fiberglass boat across a lousy ten-mile channel in clear summer weather, my Viking ancestors will disown me."

Something funny happened then. I saw her look out to sea for a moment and down at the tiny sailboat at our feet. It was hardly more than a surfboard dressed up with a mast, rudder, centerboard, and a cramped little cockpit into which you could stick your feet as you sat on the open deck a few inches above the water. In the dark, I saw the slow beginnings of a smile form at the corner of her mouth. I'd forgotten the screwball streak she'd displayed once or twice before. Suddenly she threw back her head and laughed.

"You're crazy, darling! You're absolutely insane!" There was nothing in this requiring a comment from me, so I made none. She said in a tentative voice, "I don't suppose I get to change my clothes."

That still didn't require any response. Regardless of what I'd planned earlier—or said I was planning—I'd hardly have gone to the trouble now of getting her down to the boat unseen, only to risk letting her go clear back up to her room where someone might be watching, not to mention the tricks she might play on the way. She'd given me no reason to be considerate of her or her wardrobe, and after all, what clothes were actually needed in this climate? It wasn't as if we were setting out to cross the North Sea in midwinter.

Isobel hesitated and looked down at herself in a speculative way, as if estimating what her appearance might be a couple of hours from now. Abruptly, she threw her purse into the footwell of the boat and bent over, raising her skirt garter-high. Current fashions being what they are, it didn't have far to go. A moment later she was standing there with her stockings and high-heeled pumps in her hand, having got them off with commendable speed for a lady who'd just been commenting unfavorably on the joys of going shoeless.

The reckless little half-smile on her face said she'd show me. To hell with her pretty clothes, it said: anything crazy I could do, she could do crazier. I had an uneasy feeling that she'd defeated me somehow, but I couldn't quite see how.

"Aye, aye, Skipper," she said. "Ready for launching, sir."

"Well, toss that stuff into the cockpit and let's go."

Together we dragged the boat down to the water's edge and waded out with it to where we could work on it conveniently. I saw Isobel flinch when the first wave that met us soaked her dress to the hips; after that she paid no more attention than if she'd been wearing a bikini. We checked the rudder, slipped the centerboard into its slot, hoisted the sail, and scrambled aboard. Then we were gliding smoothly away from the land, leaving five little boats where there had been six before—but I didn't think anyone was likely to count them until the beach boys arrived in the morning.

Even then, the chances of Monk's men discovering that one of the toy hotel boats was missing wasn't very great. They wouldn't be thinking in terms of cockleshells. All they would know and report, I hoped, was that Pressman was dead and that Isobel and I had disappeared mysteriously during the night.

Isobel shifted position on the deck beside me. "Ugh, if there's anything clammier than a wet bathing suit, it's a wet girdle," she said. "Matt?"

"Yes?"

"I still hate you. I loathe and despise you. I just happen to have a weakness for mad men and mad projects. Do you understand?"

I grinned. "Yes, ma'am. I'll try not to presume on your weakness, ma'am, but I guarantee nothing. Now you'd better slide that wet girdle out to windward a bit to balance us. It looks breezy up ahead. . . ."

Chapter Twenty

NOT BEING AN experienced seaman, I can't give all the technical details of the trip. The basic problem, as posed by the charts and my pocket compass, was simple enough. We wanted to sail north to Molokai, but the trade winds, which blow from the northeast in those parts, didn't really want to let us. This conflict of opinion made things quite wet and violent on board, particularly after we passed the tip of Maui and no longer had the mass of that island to shelter us.

I'd expected a certain amount of commotion, and I'd made what preparations I could. I'd collected Isobel's shoes and purse and glasses, and my shoes and gun, and rolled them up in my coat. I'd secured the bundle with my necktie and lashed it to the mast with her stockings, which lowered my popularity quotient even further. I guess no woman likes to see knots tied in her nylons. But at least we were cleared for action, so to speak, and everything was lashed down that could fall off or blow away or wash overboard when we entered the channel proper. It was just as well.

In theory, I knew, a sailboat should be able to head within about forty-five degrees, or four compass points, of the wind. In other words, with a northeast wind blowing, our northerly course was theoretically possible. This much I remembered from what I'd been taught by the old Navy chief who'd run the small-boat training school I'd attended at Annapolis years ago. I could recall him explaining to us exactly why a sailboat goes to windward. He'd drawn the parallelogram of forces on the blackboard for us. Then he'd taken us out for practical instruction, one by one, and I remembered his simple directions for sailing close-hauled, as it's called: *Just hike your ass out to weather, sir, and watch your luff.*

It had seemed a relatively simple procedure in a good-sized sailboat on the sheltered waters of Chesapeake Bay in broad daylight. On a fiberglass shingle in the Pailolo Channel at night, with the trade winds blowing across a thousand miles of open ocean and the waves marching out of the darkness mast-high, it got considerably more complicated. Well, I don't suppose they were really mast-high, and it wasn't much of a mast anyway, but after pounding into the stuff for over an hour and capsizing once, I began to have some doubts as to the feasibility of the voyage on which I'd embarked.

I mean, there's something very discouraging—not to say frightening—about clinging to an overturned boat in the dark in the middle of nowhere, even when you know perfectly well it won't sink and you'll be able to get it upright again as soon as you catch your breath from the ducking. The water was reasonably warm; there was no question of dying of exposure. Nevertheless I began to have a nagging suspicion that those old Polynesians with their hollow logs might just possibly have been better men than I.

It was then, as we rolled the boat back on its bottom and squirmed aboard, that I heard Isobel give her kookie little laugh once more.

"Darling, you're absolutely the world's worst sailor!" she shouted. "Let me take her."

"What?"

"We're not making any headway. Move over. Give me the tiller. Let me show you. . . . All right, *don't* trust me. But you're pinching her to death."

"What the hell does that mean?" I yelled. "Pinching whom?"

"The boat. You're frustrating the poor thing terribly. You're trying to make her point much too high. You've got that silly little lateen sail sheeted in so hard it can't draw properly, and you won't let it out an inch: that's why we flipped just now. And every time she does get some way on her, you run her up into the wind and stop her dead!"

It was a surprising amount of nautical lingo to come

from the lips of a decorative pillar of society, even a thoroughly wet one. However, I didn't have time to figure out the implications at the moment. A wave broke over the bow and sluiced along the deck on which we sat, half filling the cockpit. There was some kind of bailing device working down there, but for a minute or two the little vessel handled sluggishly with the extra weight of water, and I had my hands full keeping her under control.

Then I pulled my compass out of my pocket and nudged my companion to draw her attention to the luminous needle. "We've got to steer north, don't we?" I shouted. "Molokai's north, not northwest."

I heard her laugh again. "Darling, you can't work a sailboat by compass! You've got to sail by the wind and the sea. Molokai's over thirty miles long; we're not going to miss it. Once we're there, in protected water, we can make up whatever we've lost to leeward. But you're not sailing a racing yacht, Matt, with a deep lead keel and lots of momentum. You're sailing a centerboard skimming dish. To hell with pointing, you've got to keep her footing. Slack that sheet and bear off. Let her drive, or we'll be splashing around here all night."

Again, the seagoing jargon had a strange sound, considering the source, but this was hardly the place to worry about it. I hesitated only a moment. She could be tricking me somehow, but what the hell, I couldn't do worse than I was doing. I remembered that on land a sheet may be a piece of cloth, but on the water it's a rope—excuse me, a line. I let some of the nylon cord that controlled the sail slip through my hand. I pulled on the tiller, and felt the little boat swing and steady, and take off slantingly down the back of a wave like an eager pony.

Rising, she shouldered the oncoming crest aside and made the swift downward rush again, almost planing. I felt a hand take hold of the nylon line to which I clung, and I looked quickly at the woman beside me.

"At least let me tend sheet for you," Isobel shouted. "Now you're getting the idea. Just keep her driving!"

That was all there was to it—except about four more hours of wind and spray. It was still dark when we reached Molokai, feeling the motion ease as we sailed into the lee of the island. Presently I spotted the flash of breakers ahead, and made out the solid mass of the mountains against the starry black sky. It took us a while to beat around the end of the island against the wind. We felt the full blast of the trades again, rounding the easternmost point of land, but pretty soon we were able to swing away from it and run more or less downwind, really flying. The sky was getting light behind us. The forbidding north coast of Molokai began to open up to our left.

I headed into the first bay I saw, but there was a station wagon parked on the sandy beach—fishermen perhaps—and a road wound up the cliff behind it. I remembered Jill telling me about the road that went just around the end of the island and no farther: I'd obviously headed in too soon. I steered back out, and let a couple of minor openings go past, and managed to jibe and dunk us once more as I turned in again. As Isobel had suggested, I was undoubtedly the worst sailor ever to visit this coast.

We knew our vessel pretty well by now, however, and it took us only a moment to right her, scramble back aboard, and get her going again. Then we were sailing into a deep cove between towering black cliffs. There was a pretty bit of white beach at the end and a stream. Lush jungle led back up a spectacularly beautiful valley to high mountains boasting a sparkling waterfall just touched by the first rays of the sun.

I mean, it was an unreal place and an unreal situation. Coming there by motorboat properly equipped for exploration would have been one thing. Sailing up to the beach on a glorified surfboard, with nothing but the clothes we'd put on for dinner the night before, was something else again. It was crazy enough to give the whole business a vague, dreamlike quality.

I pulled up the centerboard. We slid off into the water on opposite sides of our faithful little ship and carried

her reverently up on shore. Then we turned to face each
other in the growing light. There were all kinds of questions still to be settled between us, but one thing was
certain: between us we'd licked the Pacific Ocean, or a
small part of it. That was a bond that couldn't be ig-
nored.

Isobel made a gesture of pushing the tangled wet hair
out of her eyes. In a sense, I knew her very well after
what we'd just been through together. In another sense,
she was an utter stranger, standing there barefoot with
her careful makeup washed away and her expensive cocktail dress soaked and disorganized. The funny thing was,
she looked kind of soft and pretty and appealing that
way. In the tropics, I realized, being wet wasn't really a
social disaster, particularly on a deserted beach at daybreak. You merely had to discard a few stodgy, civilized
notions about smoothly ironed dresses and sharply
creased pants.

"Well, we made it," Isobel said in a strangely gentle
voice. "You and your Viking ancestors! If you'd been
aboard, Leif Ericson would surely have drowned before
he got halfway to Vinland."

I grinned. "Why is it that the most insufferably con-
ceited people in the world are invariably those who've
managed to learn the difference between a sheet and a
halyard?"

What we were saying had, of course, nothing to do
with what we were thinking; and what we were thinking—what I was thinking, at least—had very little to do
with danger and duty and my reasons for coming here
in the first place. To hell with Monk. If he wanted me,
he could come and get me, and save me the trouble of
searching for him.

In the meantime, there was other business to be trans-
acted. Tired and bruised as we both were after the long,
rough sail, we still knew what this place was for. I mean,
who can mistake the Garden of Eden? But there had
been some misunderstandings in the past and we had to
feel our way.

I said rather tritely, like any movie hero confronted

by a damp movie heroine, "Well, you'd better get out of those wet clothes while I scout around a bit."

She smiled at this. "Don't be corny," she murmured. "I'm not cold. I'll be dry in a few minutes, as soon as the sun gets up a little higher." Her smile grew stronger. "If you really want my dress off, Matt, you'll have to think up a better reason."

I did.

Chapter Twenty-one

IT WAS HIGHLY unprofessional behavior, of course, and it would undoubtedly have served me right if I'd been caught there playing Adam to dark-haired Eve on an open beach in broad daylight, but I wasn't. Afterward I did what I should have done first: I hid the boat carefully up the stream, and I scouted around for traces of hostile life forms—or any human life at all.

I reflected on what a ridiculous, impulsive, schoolboy act it had been, but I didn't think of it with any great amount of shame or regret. Hell, I'd got away with it, hadn't I? And after all, I was more or less planning on getting myself caught, somehow, although not necessarily here and preferably with my pants on.

There were no indications that any human being had passed this way since the invention of the beer bottle and the tin can. The little inlet quickly dwindled to a jungle brook that was definitely no secret small-boat harbor, and the valley was too narrow to hide any sinister installations. K was apparently farther down the coast, maybe just around the cliff to the west, maybe miles away.

All I found was a couple of talkative mynah birds, a lot of brilliant flowers, and a pretty pool with some fish in it, reminding me that I was getting hungry. Unfortunately, hunting is my sport; I've never been much of a fisherman. While I stood there, considering the problem,

I heard Isobel's voice.

"Matt? Matt, where are you?"

"Up here," I called. "Just follow the creek."

She came into sight on the other bank, carrying some gear that seemed to be mostly mine—I'd put on only my shoes and slacks for exploring.

"Damn you, don't run off like that," she said a little breathlessly. "I was starting to get worried. This is a lovely spot, darling, but I'd rather not have it *all* to myself. Here are your things; they're practically dry." She dumped her burden by a rock and looked down at the clear water. "It looks almost good enough to drink. Is it?"

I shrugged. "I've been sampling it. It hasn't killed me yet."

She knelt on the rock and bent over to drink from her cupped hands. Straightening up, she dried her hands on her dress in a slightly defiant way, as if to emphasize that she was a nature girl now, and no longer the fastidious, well-groomed lady of yesterday. Well her dress was hardly the smooth, bright, smart silk sheath of yesterday either. However, considered just as a garment and not as a status symbol, it had sustained remarkably little real damage. It was sea-stained and badly faded, of course, and it had a puckered and rough-dried look, but it was essentially intact: it even retained a hint of style in the provocative draping of the bodice.

In a way, it was disappointing. I mean, this was just the spot for some real shipwrecked-looking, peekaboo, desert-island-type rags. By way of partial compensation was the fact that she quite obviously wasn't wearing a damn thing but her dress and shoes and glasses. I guess she'd left the rest of her stuff hanging up to dry somewhere.

I said, "Lady, you're not decent. If you don't watch out, bending over like that, you're going to fall right out of the top of that beat-up garment."

She sighed: "The man's insatiable. . . . If they arouse you so violently, darling, why don't you come over here and do something about it." When I made no move to accept this wanton challenge, she laughed and looked down at herself with clinical interest. "My husband should see me now. He has an idea that I'm incapable of existing more than a hundred feet from a beauty parlor."

I said, "This is a hell of a time to be talking about husbands."

I waded over to her and sat down on the rock beside her. We didn't speak for a little. Presently she slipped off her still damp pumps, with a sigh of relief, and dipped her feet in the pool. There are areas of the female anatomy that fascinate me more than feet, but she looked kind of cute sitting there like a kid, trailing her toes in the water. It scared me to realize once more that I was getting quite fond of her. I cleared my throat and started to say something businesslike, to dispel the dreamy atmosphere of the place, but she was already speaking.

"Do you want to know a funny thing, Matt," she said very quietly. "Don't laugh, but I'm happy. It won't last, of course, but for the moment I feel beautifully irresponsible and very happy. I don't have to worry if my stockings are straight or the bank account is overdrawn. I don't have to wonder what we're going to do when Kenneth puts it all on the red and the black comes up. It's not that I'm in love with you, darling, you understand that, of course."

"Sure," I said. "Of course."

"I think you're a nice enough man in your way—a kind of cold-blooded and ruthless way. Did you really kill those men you were scaring me with last night? No, don't tell me, I don't really want to know. And you're certainly a brave man or a very foolhardy one to put to sea on a poker chip without knowing how to sail. And making love with you is very pleasant, and being here without you wouldn't be the same thing at all. But that doesn't mean I'm yearning to marry you and spend the rest of my life mending your socks and shoulder holsters."

"I told you," I said. "I don't wear them. Holsters, I mean."

She patted my arm, smiling. "Am I hurting your feelings, Matt? Isn't it enough that I'm happy for a moment in this crazy place? Do I have to pretend to be passionately mad for you, too?" She laughed quickly, as if embarrassed, and spoke in normal tones: "And if anybody'd ever told me that one day I'd be sitting on a rock in the jungle with a wrinkled dress and stringy hair and no undies on, talking sentimentally about happiness. . . . !" She broke off and drew a long breath. "Hadn't you better do something about that gun?"

"What?"

I'd actually forgotten about the weapon. I don't forget loaded guns, but my subconscious mind apparently refused to be bothered with keeping close track of a gun that wouldn't really shoot.

"Your gun, Mr. Secret Agent," Isobel said. "There in the jacket I just brought you. It got all wet and salty, remember?" She reached down and picked up the wrinkled coat and pulled out the revolver and looked at it curiously. "How do you break it, Matt?"

I said, "Throw it against a rock. Or hit it with a hammer. It's a very light model. You ought to be able to smash it without too much trouble."

She made a face at me. "Don't make fun of me, just because I used the wrong word. I meant, how do you open it?"

"You push the latch at the side and swing the cylinder out. . . . That's the way."

"Why, it only holds five. I thought they all had six shots. Will it shoot after being wet?"

"Sure it'll shoot." The lie made me feel a little guilty, and I went on quickly, "Modern ammunition is pretty well waterproof and oilproof."

She snapped the cylinder back into place. "How do you work it?"

"You put a big wad of cotton in each ear, and then you hold it out right-handed—if you are right-handed—and brace your right hand with your left and pull the trigger back smoothly until all hell breaks loose. You do that five times. Then you throw the thing away and get a baseball bat and walk up and hit the guy on the head until he dies."

She laughed. "You don't seem to have a great deal of faith in the tools of your trade, Mr. Helm." She used a corner of her skirt to wipe the weapon clean. "How far will it shoot? Accurately, I mean?"

"Having worked at it for a few years, I might be able to hit a man at fifty yards if he stood real still. You probably couldn't hit a man at ten feet, unless you were lucky." She made me nervous, playing with the gimmicked gun, or I probably wouldn't have said it: "Or unless you're faking."

She glanced at me quickly. "Faking?"

I asked flatly, "Just what is this thing you have about guns, Mrs. Marner?"

"I don't know." Her voice was cool now. "What is this thing you have about bosoms, Mr. Helm? Guns make me feel all funny inside. I've always wanted to know how to use one, but whenever I asked somebody, they thought I was joking or planning to murder my husband. Maybe it's a fetish I have, or something. They're such perfect phallic symbols, aren't they?"

I grinned. "You really are a screwball. Put that phallic symbol down before you hurt somebody with it."

She laid it gently on top of my jacket. She wasn't smiling. She drew a long breath. "Well, now we know, don't we?" she murmured.

"Know what?"

"You weren't quite sure I wasn't going to turn it on you. Were you?"

I said, "Any experienced man is afraid of a gun in the hands of a novice or a kook, doll. But okay, let's put the cards on the table. Am I supposed to have implicit faith in you now, just because we've made beautiful music under a tropical sky? Am I supposed to forget that you trafficked, as the saying goes, with my enemies?"

She said, "Those enemies were U.S. agents, Matt." Before I could speak, she went on swiftly, "I asked you!

Remember that I asked you. You wouldn't tell me. If I couldn't get the answer from you, I had to get it from them, didn't I?"

I looked at her for a moment. "How did you know they were American agents?"

"I . . . I played detective. At that porpoise place. When you were talking to that boy, the one you put to sleep later, I sneaked up behind the tree and listened. I had to. You wouldn't tell me what was going on. I had to know what I was getting involved in. And you or he, I don't remember which, said something to indicate that you were all American agents. Only you had done something bad, something to make the others watch you and follow you. That's why I asked you that, later. Whether . . . whether I'd be a traitor to my country if I helped you. And you wouldn't tell me."

I said grimly, "But Pressman was glad to tell you, I have no doubt. And of course you believed him. And spilled your guts to him."

She licked her lips. "I had to, Matt. Everything fitted. Everything except the fact that I rather liked you."

I sighed. "You know, Duchess, the funny thing about this racket, full of suspicion and deceit, is how many times you just damn well have to haul off and take somebody on faith. But all right. You tricked me and I tricked you. We're even. Now if you still want to hear the words said, I'll say them. But first tell me one thing: where did you learn to sail?"

"Well, we do a bit of it around San Francisco, but I learned on Chesapeake Bay, when I was a child. I told you I was born there."

"It's a good place for it. That's where I picked up what little I know. Then you are Isobel Marner?"

"Yes, of course." She looked startled. "Did you really think I wasn't?"

"When I saw you playing footsie with the opposition, I didn't know what to think. Okay. Now what do you want to know?"

In response to her questions, I told her everything I dared, everything that wouldn't involve anybody else in danger, if she let something slip later or was made to talk. When I'd finished, she shook her head in a bewildered way.

"All this, so many people dead, and you still don't know where you're going, or what you'll be trying to stop when you get there! Why, you don't even know that Mr. Rath—this man you call Monk—is up to anything very reprehensible."

"Sure," I said. "He shoved Naguki off the Pali just for laughs. And he's just playing Chinese checkers with these experts from Peking. I know the Monk, doll. If it's his, it's big and nasty." I grimaced. "As for where I'm going, I was hoping to get that out of you."

"Out of *me?*"

"Why do you think I brought you along?" I grinned at her. "I told you I had a use for you, remember? And you certainly did come in handy, but I didn't know how well you could sail when we started out. I just figured if you were in cahoots with Pressman, you probably knew the location of K. And anything a girl knows, a girl can be made to tell."

She stared at me, aghast. "You mean . . . you mean you really brought me here to beat me up?" Then, surprisingly, she began to laugh. "Oh, darling, you're wonderful! Maybe I am a little in love with you, after all. When I think of all those creepy little frightened men with their creepy little country club intrigues . . . Matt."

"Yes?"

"What are you going to do now? Shouldn't you be, well, doing *something?* I mean, besides watching the top of my poor bedraggled dress, hoping I'll fall out."

"I am doing something," I said. "I'm trying to figure out how to catch that fish. He looks like a nice big tasty one. What do you know about survival-type fishing?"

She moved her shoulders. "Well, I once read a story where a girl unraveled her stockings for a line and used a bit of metal from her garter for a hook. . . ."

I heard it then. Somebody was slipping through the jungle from the west, as well as one can slip through that tangled stuff. Somehow we'd been spotted sailing in here, and now the fish—the big fish—was taking the bait I'd offered him: me. I wouldn't have to go through the motions of looking for him, after all. He was coming looking for me.

I said casually, "Well, we can give it a try. I'm getting pretty damn hungry. I think your stockings are still on the boat, keeping company with my necktie. Where'd you hang up your intimate garments?"

She told me. She seemed intrigued by the project. "I'm afraid the garter stuff is all plastic nowadays," she said, "but there's a wire in my bra we can use. Matt, be serious. What are you going to *do*?"

I leaned over to kiss her, and gave her ungirdled behind a disrespectful slap that I'd never have presumed to apply to the smoothly controlled derriere of yesterday's aloof and dignified Mrs. Marner. I hoped the byplay looked nice and casual to the man out in the brush.

"Relax, doll," I said. "Food first. Now just stay put; don't go wandering off and getting lost. Isobel. . . ."

"What is it, Matt?"

"I'm glad you were happy, if only for a moment. Sorry I had to get suspicious and spoil it."

Her eyes searched my face, suddenly questioning. I shouldn't have got sentimental; she was smart enough to guess there was trouble on the way. I could see that she wanted to look around uneasily, but she restrained the impulse. Instead she just smiled and patted my arm. I walked away quickly, wanting to put as much distance between us as possible before they lowered the boom on me, one way or another.

It happened just as I reached the edge of the clearing, but not the way I'd expected. The way it happened was my fault. I'd forgotten that damn gimmicked gun again. I'd left it lying right there on my coat in plain sight, not thinking much about it one way or another, since I knew it wouldn't shoot—but, of course, Isobel didn't know that, and neither did the prowler in the woods.

I heard the snap of a breaking branch out there, and I heard Isobel jump up and cry a warning as sunlight flashed on bright metal among the leaves. Maybe she was just defending herself instinctively. Maybe she was defending me. Or maybe it was that thing she had about guns: here was her chance, at last, to shoot one.

Whatever the reason, she went for the sawed-off revolver on the ground and got it into her hands—both hands, the way I'd told her—and started to aim it, kneeling there.

The gun in the jungle fired only once.

Chapter Twenty-two

ALMOST THE FIRST thing you learn in this business is to hell with the dead and wounded. I heard the pistol fire. I heard the bullet strike. I heard Isobel gasp and fall. Rushing back to cradle her in my arms and shake my fist at the hidden sniper would have looked great on TV, but it wasn't really practical. As a matter of fact, I never even paused to consider it. I was heading in the other direction.

I hit the tangled stuff hard and went through it like a bulldozer. There are two ways of handling a situation like that. Either you spend all day at it, sneaking around like an Indian trying to catch the guy at a disadvantage, or you rush him right now. I had only my little knife against his gun, but in the jungle that wasn't as great a handicap as it would have been elsewhere. He wouldn't see me, anyway, until I was right on top of him.

I dove into the vines and brush, swung left, and fought my way toward the spot from which the shot had come. I wouldn't have tried it against an automatic weapon, of course, or even against a shotgun. With a good spread of lead you can shoot at sounds with some hope of hitting the guy who made them. But with the revolver I'd glimpsed, the guy couldn't just spray the jungle and hope; he didn't have that much firepower. He probably didn't have that much ammunition, either.

He had to wait until he saw me over the sights at close range, and hope to make the first shot good.

I caught a hint of movement in the brush ahead. He was sneaking off to the right, away from the pool and the motionless body on the ground. I got an impression of a gaudy red-and-yellow Hawaiian shirt and white pants, almost the same costume Hanohano had been wearing. Maybe it was an omen. I didn't stop to figure out whether it was good or bad.

I just gave a loud yell and charged, screaming like a Comanche in full war paint. I mean, there was no chance of his not hearing me coming through that stuff, and people do get nervous, waiting for a clear shot at a howling wild man. Besides, there's a theory to the effect that the louder you shout the better you fight. Anyway, I just felt like yelling. Maybe I was mad.

I broke through the brush and saw my target right there. The gun was my target. I didn't even look at the guy holding it; I focused on the weapon. I had to put it out of action before it killed me; and an instant before I figured the shot was due, I dove in low, beneath the probable course of the bullet. My shoulder cut the guy down, and my hand reached up and got the wrist as we fell together. I slammed the hand and arm against a convenient tree, and the thing was done. Nothing remained but to cut the murdering bastard's throat and smile at him pleasantly as he died.

"Matt! Matt, please. It's me, Jill! *Matt, don't . . .* !"

The voice seemed to come from a long way off. I guess I had been a bit mad, at that. I drew a long breath and sat up, looking at what I had there, pinned to the ground. It was Jill, all right, in sneakers and a pair of those white jeans that are running the blue ones off the market, although I can never see why. Who wants to be washing jeans all the time?"

Hers needed washing badly, I noticed. As a matter of fact, with her muddy pants, torn shirt, and tangled hair, she was well qualified to join our castaways' club—and there was a probable opening in the membership, now.

I said harshly, "What the hell are you doing here? Besides shooting people in the back, I mean?"

"Matt, I couldn't help it! She had a gun; she was going to shoot. What could I do?"

"She couldn't have hit you with a sawed-off shotgun and a full box of twenty-five shells."

"How could I know that? How do you know that? Anyway, I didn't shoot her in the back. Are you going to sit on me all day?" I got up slowly. I folded my knife and put it away, while Jill rose and brushed herself off. She said with an effort at lightness, "When you come, Eric, you really come, don't you? I tried to call to you, to tell you who I was, but you were making so much noise you didn't hear me."

"You might have called before shooting, instead of afterward." I pawed around in the vines and leaves until I found her gun, another one of those stainless steel jobs the Monk seemed to pass around like Christmas cards. It wasn't a bad-looking weapon, for a belly-gun. The bright finish had a look of class quite unlike nickel plating. Jill put out her hand, but I stuck the revolver into the top of my pants. "To hell with you, doll. I don't like trigger-happy people around me with guns. Let's go see how much damage you've done. You first."

She started to speak angrily, but checked herself. She licked her lips, and moved off ahead of me. Even in pants, from behind, she was a very good-looking girl, which is something many attempt and few achieve. At the moment, however, I found it hard to appreciate my fine rear view of her glorious young figure. This was the girl I'd come a long way to find, but it was hardly the reunion I'd expected.

I guess what really bugged me—aside from the simple, incomprehensible fact of her being here at all—was that I was entirely in the wrong, blaming her for what had happened. Isobel *had* picked up my gun. She *had* been about to shoot. Jill's strategy in sneaking up on us without warning might be criticized, but her reaction to the threat could not, considering how she'd been trained.

It seemed to be just one of those sickening damn-fool

things that happen when you leave guns around carelessly—and I was the guy whose gun it was, who'd left it there. If I'd taken care of my weapon as I should, the thing would never have happened.

The figure by the pool did not move as we approached. The faded, incongruous silk dress no longer seemed like a good joke on stuffy old civilization. It was just a small indignity added to the greater indignity of death. I was reasonably sure, anyway, but I knelt beside the body and lifted it gently. There was no need to turn it over completely to see the great, shiny spill of blood below the left breast. I let her down again slowly.

I knelt there for a little, holding her, telling myself I was getting too old for this work, or something. Hell, people died all the time, even attractive women. They got smashed up in cars, they got shot by jealous boyfriends, they caught diseases antibiotics couldn't cure, and if nothing else worked they took sleeping pills by the fistful in the spirit of do-it-yourself. I had a job to do, even if I still didn't quite know what it was. I shouldn't be wasting time or emotion on one lousy society dame dead on a crummy Pacific island, even if she had died kind of by mistake.

I heard Jill's young voice: "Aren't you taking this awfully big, Eric?"

She was right, of course, but I looked up at her and said, "Children should be seen and not heard. Comb your damn hair and shut your damn mouth."

She said stubbornly, "I mean, if you want me to say I'm sorry, I'll say it. But really, if you're going to make a career of this business, you can't have a spastic over every enemy agent you kill. Can you?"

I stared at her for a long moment. "Come again?"

She frowned, surprised. "You mean you didn't know? I heard them talking. I heard all about her. Her code name is—was—Irina, and she was one of Moscow's best in the Asiatic division. Maybe that's why you never came across her dossier; you never worked against that bunch, did you? She disappeared for a while and now she turns up here, calling herself first Isobel McLain and then, I gather, Isobel Marner, your loving sister-in-law. Just how they worked that I didn't hear. It may have been kind of tough on the real Isobel Marner, if any. Of course, they may simply have gambled on your being in no position to check on whether or not such a person actually exists." Jill looked down at me in a speculative, adult way. "I see you don't believe me, Eric. The woman must have been very good. Very convincing. But maybe you'll believe this. Where's her purse?"

I hesitated briefly, and jerked my head toward the battered-looking white kid purse that lay beside a pair of battered-looking white kid pumps on the nearby rock. Jill got it and opened it.

"How do you think I knew where to come?" she said. "I came here to warn you. Monk knows you're here. He's been tracking you ever since you turned Halawa Point at the end of the island early this morning. Look."

She had a familiar cigarette lighter in her hand. She slid the cover off to show me the interior mechanism. Half was what you'd expect to find inside an ordinary butane lighter, slimmed down in one dimension. The other half looked like a mass of dirty spaghetti with bugs in it, which is the way most of that fancy electronic equipment looks to the uninitiated.

"A beeper," I said softly. "By God, she was carrying a beeper all the time!"

As I spoke, I felt the woman I held stir minutely in my arms.

Chapter Twenty-three

I WASN'T QUITE aware of making the decision. The mental computer just ran the tape through on its own, and came up with an answer. Without really thinking it over consciously I found myself closing my fingers hard on Isobel's arm, warning her to lie perfectly still.

To mask the signal, I lowered her to the ground at last, making it look, I hoped, like an act of rejection.

"Well, I guess she isn't playing possum this time," I said loudly. "She fooled a couple of Monk's men that way once, pretending to be unconscious when she wasn't. At least she said she did, but I guess it was just part of the act." I gave the bare arm another sharp little squeeze to call attention to my words, and went on harshly for Jill's benefit, "I should have realized she played too smart and cool all along for the simple society bitch she was supposed to be."

Jill just dropped the lighter back into the purse, snapped the purse closed, and tossed it back onto the rock. I got up, and glanced at my hands, and wiped them on my coat. Then, as an afterthought, I tossed the coat over the woman on the ground, ostensibly as a Christian gesture, and flung my shirt over her legs to finish the job of covering the body decently. I turned to face Jill.

"All right, little girl," I said. "So the old pro is just an impressionable sucker after all. Is that why you shot her?"

"Well, I knew she was dangerous. When she went for the gun. . . ." Jill shrugged.

That reminded me that I'd forgotten the weapon once more. I just couldn't seem to keep my mind on it, any more than if it had been a toy pistol. I got it and tucked it into my pants, making room for it by taking out Jill's silvery weapon and giving it back to her apologetically.

"Sorry I was rough on you. I suppose you had to play it cagey, sneaking up on us. You couldn't know how she'd react."

"That's right, Matt. I knew she'd probably guess I'd picked up enough information to expose her. I had to take her by surprise. I'm sorry it worked out so badly. I . . . I'm not really very experienced at this sort of stuff, you know."

The little hesitation was very convincing. I regarded the girl thoughtfully, noting that her gaudy shirt had lost a strategic button and most of a sleeve, but that it looked just a little like the kind of phony-ragged garment, art-fully tattered with scissors, that you'd wear to a masquerade. I was willing to bet, now, that she'd smeared the mud on her jeans with her own hands, to emphasize the hardships she'd endured to reach me. But she was still a lovely thing, with her fine tan and her striking blonde hair and her frank blue eyes. It was just too bad she was a goddamn liar.

Either that or she'd been deceived, although it was hard to see how it could have been done. Or I was the world's biggest sucker, because I didn't believe a word she'd said against Isobel. I mean, as I'd said earlier, there are times in this faithless business when you've simply got to haul off and have a little faith in somebody.

What it amounted to was that I had to choose. I had to choose between the tall blonde girl who sounded very convincing and had a trick cigarette lighter for evidence, and the slim dark-haired woman who'd said to me softly, *"Matt, don't laugh, but I'm happy."* I could believe that the woman who'd said that, in the way she'd said it, was exactly what she'd claimed to be, or I could believe that she was the world's most consummate actress.

I didn't think they came that good. And the cigarette lighter didn't really count. It could have been planted in her purse at any time, without her knowledge. They're made by the millions, they burn for months, and one looks just like another—at least, a duplicate wouldn't have been hard to find. For a choice, the switch had been made when Francis and his sidekick searched her room, mauling her in the process. There had never been a really good explanation for that whole clumsy performance until now; and Francis had been trying to warn me about something in this connection when he died.

I could have misunderstood the warning. He could have been trying to warn me against the lighter, instead of against the person who carried it.

In any case, I'd made my choice. I was putting my money on the woman on the ground. I was gambling that she was exactly what she'd said: Isobel Marner, from Frisco, Cal., although they don't like that name up there.

I was betting on her screwball streak, and on the guts she'd displayed in the Pailolo Channel.

I was also gambling, of course, that she wasn't so badly hurt she'd go and die on me after all. Actually, I told myself, the amount of blood I'd seen could be considered a good sign rather than a bad one. They don't generally bleed like that when they're shot through the lungs or heart. Most often, in such cases, the hemorrhage stays internal and all you see outside is a small, red-rimmed hole. Copious bleeding there indicated a flesh wound, a nasty, open bullet furrow along the ribs, perhaps, very painful and messy but seldom fatal.

I was betting my life, and perhaps a lot of other people's lives—depending on what Monk had in mind—that she was not too badly injured to be listening now, and that she'd be strong enough and smart enough and brave enough to understand my instructions and follow them. It was a lot to ask of a sheltered woman, inexperienced in violence, and badly hurt. It was a lot to ask of anybody, but I had to give it a try.

Of course, I would have preferred to rush over and bandage her tenderly and load her into the boat and get her to a doctor—but then, I'd also have preferred to be somewhere far away, taking the vacation that was coming to me. My preferences were strictly irrelevant. If Isobel could play possum well enough and listen hard enough, she could be useful; if not, I'd have to do my job without her help. In neither case was I here to make like Florence Nightingale: she'd have to patch up her own damn holes. I was leaving her my shirt to do it with. Our jungle idyll was over and it was time to go to work.

I said to Jill, "Okay, kid. Give it to me fast. What have you learned? First of all, where's K?"

"It's over there about five miles," she said, pointing. "Down the coast to the west. Not the next bay but the one after that. It would be easy enough in a boat, but it's kind of a rough trip overland, everything from gooey swamps and jungle to sharp lava rocks. Well, look at me! Matt, I—"

"You say Monk knows I'm here. What's he doing about it?"

"Nothing, at the moment. They're all busy working on the boat. He figures, with the woman to watch you, and her transmitter to show when you change position, you'll keep until he's got a couple of men free to go after you. Of course, once he learns I'm missing. . . ."

"That's the next question," I said. "Just why the hell are you missing? I told you to get to K and stay put. I told you I'd find you."

"But I had to warn you!" she protested. "I had to let you know you were walking into a trap, with a traitor at your back. Didn't I? Matt . . ."

I said, "Maybe I wanted to walk into a trap. Maybe that's why I sent you on ahead, so you'd be there to get me out of it. Next time, Jill, just follow instructions and don't worry so damn much about other people's safety. Little angels of mercy we can do very well without."

Her eyes flashed angrily, but her voice was humble. "Yes, Matt. I'm sorry if I made a mistake. I thought it was the thing to do."

So I knew she was a phony—a lovely, hypocritical phony—and not just an innocent girl being used as a patsy in some clever Monkish way. Well, she'd always been kind of a question mark; I'd even commented to Mac about the inconsistency of a girl who looked like a tall young goddess and acted like a small white mouse.

It remained to be seen whether she was a truly sinister and complex person, much more deeply involved in Monk's intrigues than anyone could have guessed, or whether she'd simply been caught, exposed, and frightened into changing sides. There are a good many threats that can be used against a pretty girl, particularly one with no great reputation for courage, and Monk would know them all.

"Well, we'll just have to refigure the program," I said easily. "Can you lead me there in such a way that we're not spotted? Or maybe you can just tell me how to find the place and get past the guards—I suppose he does have guards out."

Jill hesitated. "I'd better guide you. I can save you some time and a lot of nasty climbing and wading, and I know where Monk's men are posted. Matt—"

"And now for the big question," I said. "What's he up to? Have you been able to learn that?"

"Of course I have!" she said quickly. "That's what I've been trying to tell you. Matt, it's horrible. It's the *General Hughes*!"

"The what?"

"The *Hughes*. The *General Herman Hughes*. The transport, Matt. The troop transport!"

I looked at her for a moment, but I was thinking of the boys with the dog tags I'd seen on the beach. They hadn't impressed me too favorably. In my book, punks who lounge around making audible comments about strangers should have their tails kicked up between their ears, in the armed forces or out. Nevertheless, I didn't particularly want anything more drastic to happen to them. Hell, there might even be a nice, quiet, respectful young fellow in the lot, and we couldn't risk losing such a rare specimen.

"I see," I said softly. "I see. I presume he's going to sink it?" She nodded. I asked, "How? No, don't tell me. It's the Monk, so he'll blow it up dramatically. Lots of noise and smoke and flame. He likes big bangs. Particularly big bangs with people inside them."

Jill nodded again. "Yes, of course. The explosives have already been planted on the ship."

"Where? I mean, is he using limpet mines of some kind stuck to the outside of the hull, or did they smuggle the stuff aboard somehow?"

"I . . . I don't know where it is. I just know that end of the job has been taken care of to everybody's satisfaction."

"Okay," I said. "Now, how's he planning to detonate, with a timing device or something? No, it wouldn't be that, not with the Monk. He likes to push his own buttons and see them blow. How has he got it rigged?"

"I don't know the technical details, Matt, but it's a radio-type gadget in one of the boats. The bigger one, the inboard-outboard. They're fixing it up for the skis now. That's how I got to K. He needed somebody to ride them, somebody who . . . who'd look good in a bikini."

I looked at her sharply. "You're going a little too fast for me. Skis?"

"Yes. Water skis. Don't you see? Who'll suspect a speedboat towing a . . . a pretty girl with long blonde hair, on water skis? Why, the boys will line the rails and whistle and hoot and throw down the leis the girls gave them in town, as we come alongside. And then . . . and then, after we've swung off to a safe distance, Monk will push the button. . . ." We didn't say anything for a little. I didn't look toward the coat-covered shape by the rock. Presently Jill went on dully, "They made it easy for him, docking in Honolulu instead of Pearl Harbor. They leave early tomorrow morning, and tomorrow's Saturday. That means the *Lurline* will be coming in. That means the whole ocean will be full of boats anyway, waiting to greet the liner. One more won't attract any attention at all. Even after the explosion, Monk figures, we won't be noticed particularly. Everybody'll be watching the *Hughes*."

"What happens then?"

"We just slip away in the confusion and rendezvous somewhere—I don't know where—with the other boat, the one with no incriminating gadgets on board. We'll switch boats and head out to meet a getaway ship. I haven't learned the details of that. Monk said leave it all to him. He . . . he thinks I'm in love with him. He thinks I'm doing it all, not only for my political beliefs, but because I want to go away with him. I . . . I had to let him think that." She was blushing a little. I wasn't as impressed as I might have been if I hadn't seen her instant blush before.

I said, "And what about his political beliefs? Just why is he doing all this?"

"Isn't it obvious? To protest against the war, of course. And to keep all those troops from getting there to fight."

I said, "It doesn't sound like the Monk to me. He never impressed me as the peaceful type. Of course he may have got soft in his old age, but what about this lady from Moscow? I can see how the Peking bunch got into the act, if he needed technical assistance, although the Monk I used to know wouldn't have needed anybody's help with explosives and detonators. But what's a Russki agent doing here? You did say she was Moscow, didn't you?"

"Yes, of course, but I don't know what her function is. Does it matter? Those communists all work together, don't they?"

I laughed. "Don't bet your life on it. Well, if you don't know, you don't know." I frowned. "This changes things a bit. We've got to get word to Honolulu somehow. There's a boat hidden over there in the reeds; that's your baby. First give me directions to K. I'll do what I can there. But you take that boat and hide it somewhere else until dark, so it won't be found when Monk's men come prowling around. Then you put to sea and steer west towards Kalaupapa, the leper colony. It shouldn't be more than a two or three hours' run downwind, if the trades blow as hard as they did last night. There's a lighthouse at the end of the Kalaupapa peninsula, according to the chart. You can home in on that. Swing around it and land on the leeward side of the peninsula. That seems to be where most of the installations are. They'll have communications equipment available. Make sure the word gets to Honolulu right away. That ship mustn't sail tomorrow. Okay?"

I spoke as loudly and clearly as I could without arousing Jill's suspicion. I was careful not to look toward Isobel. There was no sign of life under my coat and shirt. I wondered if I'd misinterpreted the faint stirring I'd felt.

Well, either she was alive or she wasn't. Either she'd heard or she hadn't. Either she'd get word to Kalaupapa or she wouldn't. I couldn't do it. If I put to sea now, the lookouts would spot me from K, just down the coast, and the speedboats would run me down within a mile. If I tried to cross the mountains to the south on foot. I might take days trying to find my way through the jungles and up the spectacular precipices this volcanic geology seemed to favor. We didn't have that much time.

And if I just waited for darkness, the Monk would come after me long before I could slip away unseen. My best bet was to keep him away from this place by going to him. That gave Isobel an escape, if she was strong enough to use it; and it might put me in a position for some judicious sabotage, if I was smart enough to take advantage of it. Of course, I had to get Jill away from here, too, but I didn't think she was going to make it hard for me, and she didn't.

She said, hesitantly, "Well, all right, Matt, but—"

"But what?"

"There's lot of time before dark. At least let me guide you part way, far enough that I can point out to you. . . . Let me feel I haven't altogether fallen down on this job. Then I'll come back and take care of the boat."

I shrugged. "Sure. Whatever you say. Just so you've got the directions clear. Straight downwind to Kalaupapa as soon as it's dark. . . ."

There were, of course, no goodbyes. I didn't even glance back; I just followed the girl away from the quiet jungle pool, out of the thick stuff, and up over the lava rocks of the promontory to the west. It was a healthy climb and the day was bright and warm; I was glad I'd started this job with a pretty good tan or I'd have been well cooked without my shirt. We were both perspiring freely by the time we got far enough around the point to see into the next bay.

It was a little larger than the one we'd left, the valley above it was wider, and the inlet looked deeper. There was no sparkling fall of water down the mountains behind it. It wasn't quite the Garden of Eden that Isobel and I had found, but then, this was no longer dawn and a lot of things had happened and Paradise was a long way off.

I could see no sign of human life ahead as I followed Jill around the point until the harsh black rocks gave way to tropical vegetation again. Here she stopped and turned to face me.

"It's just over that next ridge," she said, pointing. "You'll have to cross at the high saddle, there. A man is standing watch just below. You'll be able to make out the others, one on the next point, and one up on a kind of cliff behind the camp. If you cut well back, crossing this valley, you won't have as much trouble with the swampy stuff as I did." She grinned. "Luckily, there are no water snakes on Hawaii, or any other snakes, for that matter. You don't have to worry about that."

I regarded her for a moment. You never quite know if you're right, of course. It's always a throw of the dice, a flip of the coin. She was a very attractive young lady, even in her dirty boy's clothes. She stuck out her hand abruptly.

"I . . . I'd better get back and hide that boat, Matt."

"Sure." We shook hands. "Have a good sail, kid."

"I'll send some help. Right away."

I shook my head. "Better wait till you're sure the ship is safe, before you let them disturb things around here. I may be able to jimmy the works somehow, but not if they come charging up clumsily and spook him. We don't want to take any chance of both the detonator boat and the ship getting loose on the same ocean. Your job is the ship. I take the speedboat if I can. Make sure your job is done this time, before you worry about mine. Or me. Okay?"

She took this pompous lecture without resentment. "Yes, of course. I understand. . . . Matt?"

"What is it?"

"You don't think . . . you don't think I've done too badly, do you?"

She was really very good, or I was very wrong. I grinned, and took her shiny face in my hands, and kissed her lightly on the forehead. I felt her arms go around me impulsively, and she turned her face up for a real kiss, and got it. Then the gun was gone from my belt, and she'd jumped back, aiming it at me.

"It's all right, Monk," she called. "I have his gun. Come and get him, darling."

I raised my hands cautiously, regarding the weapon as

if I had a great deal of respect for it. Well, I'd been trying to peddle that damn castrated pistol for days. It was about time I found a taker, even though I couldn't see just how it was going to help me now.

Chapter Twenty-four

THEY WERE HIDING in the rocks: Monk and two dark-faced men in nondescript Hawaiian-type clothes, each carrying an old M-1 carbine, that bastard cross between a pistol and a rifle that I've never had any use for. However, there's no denying that under suitable conditions it will kill a man very dead.

Monk was wearing a natty khaki outfit with a short-sleeved, open-necked shirt. It looked like the latest summer uniform adopted by the armed forces, the one that makes even a four-star general look like a Boy Scout. It occurred to me that there had always been something faintly resembling an offbeat scoutmaster about the Monk. Well, the handicraft projects were different, but the burning enthusiasm was the same.

Now his blue eyes looked bright and idealistic in his sunburned, ascetic face, as he climbed down to cover me with another one of those rustless belly-guns he seemed to have got a bushel of somewhere. His helpers took my little knife and my belt, and searched me for other weapons, and found none because there were none to find.

"The same old Eric," Monk said, relaxing. "Fast with the hands, fast with the weapons, fast with the women, and very slow with the brains."

"The same old Monk," I said. "Always trying to talk people to death. If words could kill, amigo, you'd be the greatest in the business."

That got to him, because of course he did think he was the greatest in the business. Well, who doesn't? No-body'd stay in it if he didn't feel he was, in his own peculiar way, the greatest, or would be with a little more practice. We're all the greatest. The difference was that Monk could never take any kidding about it.

His eyes narrowed and he started to answer sharply, but changed his mind. Instead he just jerked his head for the two men to take me on down the path, such as it was. Jill stepped forward.

"Just a minute," she said. "I have a score to settle with this man."

Monk said irritably, "To hell with your scores, Irina. Feed your damn pride on your own damn time."

"You would not have captured him so easily without me," the girl said. "You can indulge me a little, darling. It will only take a moment." She had deliberately allowed her voice to change and become slightly foreign, and her face had changed. She was no longer the pretty, leggy, lighthearted American miss I'd been allowed to admire on the beach at Waikiki a few mornings before. She wanted me to know it. She wanted me to appreciate the skill with which she'd deceived me. Temperament we've got lots of in the trade.

She stood in front of me. "Mr. Helm."

I said, "So you're Irina, from Moscow."

She moved her shoulders briefly. "From there and elsewhere."

"I don't suppose Francis and the rest of the boys knew that."

"Those pacifist fools! They were sheep and easy to lead."

"Right into Mister Monk's slaughterhouse."

"Of course. Regularly enlisted as American agents, Mr. Helm. Don't forget that. Their records of protest will be remembered after tomorrow, as well as their official status. So will yours. You undoubtedly thought you were being clever, pretending to be of somewhat the same persuasion; you thought it might lead them to confide in you, did you not? And maybe it did, but nevertheless you played right into our hands. It is also on the record. And after you are found dead on the boat—the curiously equipped boat that will soon attract a great deal of attention—what do you think people will say about you, a man known to have been disciplined for speaking out against the war in Asia?"

I said, "So that's the gambit. Pretty tricky, Irina."

"Very tricky, Mr. Helm. Can you guess whose mad political ideas will be blamed for the horrible deaths of all those brave young American soldiers? We were going to use Naguki, of course, but then we heard that you were coming, and that you had been good enough to frame yourself much better than we could have framed Naguki. So we disposed of Naguki and concentrated on you. You thought you were being very clever, sneaking up on K by roundabout ways, but who told you about K, Mr. Helm? Who told you where to come? I did. We've been expecting you here. We've been watching your childish attempts to delude us. We've been waiting patiently for your arrival." She smiled with youthful condescension. "I'll admit that you showed admirable ruthlessness and daring in slipping away from our people on Maui last night, but the end result is the same. You are here, in our hands."

Monk said, "To hell with this, kid. If you've got something to say to him, say it."

I said to the girl, "But you're the one who tipped off Washington to the operation in the first place."

"Of course. We wanted the sheep to be rounded up, at the right time. Or found dead in the right places. We wanted a man to be sent to investigate, a man we could use. A man like Naguki, or better still, a man like you. And of course, Monk had certain private reasons for preferring you, once it was known you were coming."

Monk said, "Okay, okay, Irina. Gloating time is over."

"Just one thing more." She took a step closer to me. "Mr. Helm, do you recall a hotel room in Honolulu and a man who laughed?"

I grinned. "Sure, and you did look funny with all your clothes off, honey, asking to be laid."

She drew back her hand and slugged me hard on the side of the head with my own gun. She was a strong girl, and it was a healthy blow, almost knocking me down.

For a moment I saw nothing but flashes of light and dark. When my eyes could focus again, she was still standing there. Then she puckered up her pretty young lips and spat. Turning, she tossed the gun to Monk and marched away, her dignified exit a little spoiled—but only a little—by the mud on the seat of her jeans.

I touched the welt above my ear and felt some blood. I couldn't help wishing she'd taken it all out in spit. To the best of my knowledge, no man has been seriously damaged by saliva yet.

Monk laughed. "A woman scorned," he said.

"That's a great line," I said sourly. "I'll make a note of it, if you don't mind. You don't come across originality like that very often."

Having again made myself unpopular in that direction, too, I moved off obediently along the path the girl had taken. My head ached and I couldn't help thinking I was getting a little tired of drawing attention—sometimes misguidedly, as it turned out—away from other people at my own expense. However, I'd been afraid that if I didn't make myself so obnoxious here as to keep everybody busy hating me, they might think of sending somebody back to destroy or remove the sailboat, and perhaps even bury the body.

I wondered briefly how Isobel was making out back there, wounded and alone—if she wasn't dead—and then I dismissed her from my mind completely. While I'm not sold on extrasensory perception, I have found that if you think of something hard enough, other people often do seem to think of it, too. I didn't want anybody to think of her. Besides, I had plenty of problems of my own without worrying about hers.

I've called it a path because it was the logical route along the shore, but it wasn't the kind of manicured trail you'd find in a national park. The rough going didn't encourage conversation, but presently I asked over my shoulder, "Just what is this K bit, anyway?"

Monk had apparently decided to stop being insulted; his voice came readily enough: "Hell, you know these Hawaiian names. That's Kakananuka Bay out there. How would you like to say that twenty times a day? Besides, K sounds more mysterious and can't be located on a chart. Sweeter honey to trap the bear, Eric. And you'll have to admit you walked right into it."

"Sure." After a moment I said with careful flattery, "You must be a pretty slick diplomat, Monk. Getting Peking's Pride and the Moscow Maiden to work together must have taken some doing, considering official policies over there these days."

I heard him chuckle. "What makes you so sure they're working together, friend? Some of them may *think* they are, but—" He was interrupted by two sharp, echoing gunshots from the jungle ahead. I heard him swear. "Hell, that's a .38! Damn the trigger-happy young bitch! If she's . . . Stand right there, Eric! Put your hands behind you."

I did as I was told. Monk snapped an order at the two men accompanying us, and one of them produced a piece of cord, which Monk tested and then used to tie my wrists firmly together in back.

"These men will bring you in," he said. "Dead or alive. I'd prefer to keep you alive until tomorrow morning, but the condition of the body isn't tremendously important. It doesn't *have* to be absolutely fresh, if you know what I mean, Eric. If you want to die now, just make one bad move, and the men will be happy to oblige. I'll see you in camp. Whether you see me or not is up to you."

He pushed past me and disappeared into the leafy wilderness ahead at a run. After a moment, one of the men gave me a shove, and we followed more slowly. It was harder making progress with my hands tied, and I was too busy trying not to trip over things to watch my surroundings carefully. Anyway, Jill—or Irina, as I preferred to think of her now—had said K was over the next ridge. Like most of her information, it left a little to be desired, accuracy-wise.

Without warning, I stumbled out of the jungle into a pleasant grove of the big mesquite-*kiawes,* under which were pitched several well-camouflaged tents, carefully placed where natural growth would shield them from both air and sea observation. The flap of the nearest tent was tied back and I could see radio equipment inside. The trees ended at a placid inlet. Beyond was an open area of muck and grass and sandy hummocks.

I looked for the boats and couldn't see them at first. Then I spotted them back in the jungle to the left, where the inlet kind of disappeared into a dense tangle of vegetation. Part of this had been carefully undercut to make room along the bank—a kind of natural boathouse —for the two white speedsters.

Down at the edge of the brush, Monk was standing with Irina. There were also a couple of dark-faced, armed, Hawaiian-looking characters like the ones who formed my escort, and a chunky man in a dirty white suit. Another man, also in grubby whites, lay on the riverbank, apparently dead.

"I tell you, darling," Irina was saying angrily when we came up, "I tell you, they were trying to force their way past the guards. When I came running, that one pulled a gun. He was going to shoot; naturally I shot first."

The chunky man had a round, impassive, Oriental face and slanting dark eyes, very narrow now. His voice was soft and his English was chosen with care.

"I think I am entitled to explanation, Mr. Rath. We go to make final inspection of equipment—*our* equipment. We are seized by ruffians. My colleague is murdered by impetuous young lady. He was most valuable. My superiors will be displeased. How shall I report this unfortunate incident?"

He was a good man. He knew he was in a tight spot, a very tight spot, but his face was calm and he wasted no time on anger. He might have been discussing a defective circuit instead of a dead colleague.

"Well, Mr. Rath?" he said to Monk.

Monk's eyes were wide and grave. "I'm sorry as hell, Mr. Soo," he said—at least that's the way the name sounded to me. "I'm sorry as hell. It's a stupid misunderstanding, that's all it is. Just a misunderstanding.

You said your work was finished, so I put the boats out of bounds so no one would monkey with them until tomorrow morning. These men just take orders. They're not supposed to think; you know how it is. They didn't understand that of course *you* are free to come and go as you wish. And Miss Darnley, here, well, she's young, and nobody likes to be shot at. . . . How does it happen that your friend had a gun, Mr. Soo? I told you we would take care of all the security arrangements."

Mr. Soo, or whatever his name was, hesitated for a second or two. Then he said smoothly, "I told him it was a breach of hospitality, but he would insist on bringing it." The only sign of strain he showed was that his English, surprisingly, got a little more fluent as he talked. "So there are faults on both sides, Mr. Rath. A terrible thing, but it is done. You will take care of him?"

"Yes, of course. If you still want to look aboard the boat. . . ."

Mr. Soo smiled gently. "Not right now. I am hardly, as you say, in the mood. I will return to my tent, if you please."

He started to walk away. Monk nodded. The nearest man stepped forward and chopped him down with the butt of a carbine, using no more force than required. There was a little silence after he had fallen.

Monk looked at the man on the ground and at me. "There's your shipmate, Eric."

It was time for somebody to ask a stupid and obvious question, and I seemed to be the logical candidate. "So you and the lady from Moscow are double-crossing your Chinese associates," I said. "What the hell kind of complicated deal are you trying to pull here, Monk?"

"Not trying, friend." His eyes were bright and hot and intensely blue. "Pulling."

I glanced at the girl and looked back to Monk. "With her help. Did you sell out for rubles instead of yen, is that it?"

"Nobody sold out!" His voice was harsh. "We merely discovered, shall we say, that our interests were identical in certain areas. Large areas. When the fate of mankind is at stake, friend, one takes one's allies where one finds them! I tried to convince people in Washington, but I couldn't find anybody who'd face the facts and do what needed doing. We're governed by cowards and sentimentalists. I had to go elsewhere to find a realistic approach to international politics."

"Realistic," I said, with another glance at Irina, who kept her young face expressionless. I looked at the man she'd shot, lying there on the bank, and I remembered a woman she'd also shot, and I said, "She's realistic, all right. Are you going to tell me about this realistic approach, amigo, or do you expect me to guess?"

Monk stepped up to Mr. Soo and with his foot contemptuously rolled the unconscious Chinese over and looked down at the broad yellow face.

"There's the true enemy, Eric!" he said grimly. "They're arrogant bastards. They think they can use and outsmart anybody. They thought they could use and outsmart me. They figure civilization started with them and will end with them. And unless something's done with them soon, they may be right."

The picture was beginning to come into focus, gradually.

"And you're just the boy to do it," I murmured.

"Let's say I'm the boy to see that it gets done," Monk said. "I've spent years studying them, out here in the Pacific. They're the most dangerous people in the world, and there are more of them than there are of anybody else. Once all four hundred million of them break loose, there'll be no stopping them. We've got to do it now, Eric! Now!"

I said, "And that's what you're really working for? You're not protesting against the war we've got; quite the contrary. You're trying to promote a bigger and better one. You figure on sinking a U.S. transport with Red Chinese equipment and having the body of a Chinese technician found on board the boat that set off the explosion. You figure that will force Washington's hand. We'll have to retaliate somehow, and there'll be counter-retaliation, and what you're really hoping is that it will build up—escalate, to use the jargon—to a nuclear payoff. Is that it?"

He smiled. "You underestimate me, Eric. I've made *sure* of forcing Washington's hand. There will be found on board the boat not only a Chinese technician, but a cowardly American peacemonger fairly high in government employment. Don't forget yourself, my friend. Why do you think we were so careful to lure a man out from Washington, hoping for a fairly senior agent who, unlike the kids we'd hired for show, couldn't possibly be called a dupe or a catspaw. As Irina said, you played right into our hands with your pacifist cover. Your body found on the boat along with the Chinaman's will discredit both the pacifist groups and the wishy-washy government that tolerates them. There'll have to be action, real action, to quiet the national uproar that will follow."

I glanced at Irina. "And supposing you get your war, what part will her people take?"

Monk said, "They will fight with us. They'll have to. They have just as much to lose as we have."

"That'll be the day," I said.

"We fought together to defeat the Germans, didn't we? This is a greater danger than Hitler."

I said, "Suppose they just stand by rubbing their hands gleefully while the two largest nations they share the world with kill each other off, after which they simply move in to pick up the pieces." I didn't look at Irina, but I was aware that she'd stirred minutely, as if I'd touched a sensitive nerve. I said, "You're dreaming, Monk. I won't argue with your premise; I don't know that much about Asiatic politics. But I don't trust your allies."

"They'll have to fight," Monk said stubbornly, his eyes hard and bright. "They know as well as we do that the fate of the white race is at stake."

It startled me. I mean, I'm not particularly tolerant, and I don't really believe that everybody's equal. Depending on what I need him for, I'll judge a man by his IQ, or the score he makes on the target range, or the speed at which he can take a car around a track; and anybody who tries to tell me that some people aren't brighter than others, or better shots, or faster drivers, is wasting his time. But except for recognition purposes, I've never found the color of a man's skin to be of much significance in our line of work, and the idea of killing off a bunch of people just because of a slight chromatic difference seemed fairly irrational to me.

But what really startled me was hearing it from Monk. Not that he'd ever been particularly tolerant, either, back when I'd worked with him, but he'd subscribed to no special racial theories that I'd been aware of. But now it appeared that he'd bought the old yellow-peril package complete with paper and string, and I had a hunch I knew who'd sold it to him, although I was careful not to look toward the tall blonde girl in the muddy white jeans. I had certainly underestimated her, and by the looks of things I wasn't the only one.

Well, it was bound to happen. Somebody was bound, sooner or later, to take advantage of that strain of fanaticism that I'd always mistrusted in the Monk.

Chapter Twenty-five

DURING THE LONG AFTERNOON that followed I had plenty of opportunity to consider what I'd learned, in all its worldwide implications, but I didn't really take advantage of it. My job is a practical one and I don't feel comfortable in the rarefied atmosphere of theoretical international politics. I do hold a few private opinions about world affairs, fairly moderate ones, but I'm perfectly willing to admit they may be all haywire.

Hell, racial theories aside, maybe the Monk was right, and we should blast the Chinese off the face of the earth. Maybe we should have used the bomb on the Russians way back when we had it and they didn't. Maybe we should use it on them now, regardless. Maybe we should obliterate Castro's Cuba, or just Castro. We might even, while we were at it, do a little something about other troublesome parts of the American continents, not to mention odd areas of Africa, Asia, and Europe, if those people didn't straighten up and fly right. There were all kinds of interesting possibilities, once you started considering the idea of fixing up the world by armed force.

I wasn't qualified to say that all of them were wrong—considering my profession, I'd look silly objecting to a little judicious force—but I didn't really think the Monk was peculiarly qualified to say that one was right, not when the evidence indicated that his decision had been strongly influenced by people—one person, at least—whose motives I had no reason to trust.

In any case, it wasn't his decision any more than it was mine. I was glad I wasn't the man or men whose decision it was, but I was reasonably certain that it could be made without the help of any spectacular fireworks off Honolulu harbor.

My job wasn't to judge a political policy, it was to prevent an explosion and incidentally save a few lives—although strictly speaking, as Monk had pointed out, we're not a great, humanitarian, life-saving agency like the Red Cross or the Coast Guard. It's not, let's say, our primary objective. As a matter of fact, I recalled, my primary objective was to deal with a traitor. I concentrated on trying to figure out how to manage this, tied hand and foot on the floor of a guarded tent. I came to the conclusion that I was going to need a little luck. Well, one generally does.

I had company in the tent, of course, and presently I heard the man beside me come around to consciousness once more. His breathing changed, and he stirred briefly, testing his bonds. Having determined the nature of the predicament in which he found himself, he sensibly saved his strength and lay still.

I suppose I should have talked to him, pumped him, appealed to his pride and his sense of self-preservation, and made some kind of deal to insure his cooperation, but I didn't. I couldn't think of anything he could tell me that I needed to know at the moment, and he was too bright, I figured, not to cooperate if it seemed to his advantage to do so—and probably too unscrupulous to stick by any deals if it didn't.

Toward evening, Irina entered with food and water. I was interested to note that she'd exchanged her artfully tattered shirt for a whole one, equally gaudy. The guard stood by at the open tent door with his carbine ready while she untied the hands of Mr. Soo, let him eat and drink, and lashed him up again. Then it was my turn. She got a good deal of innocent fun out of my clumsy efforts to absorb nourishment with my feet still tied and my fingers stiff from bondage. Afterward, Monk came in to check the knots.

I said, "Aren't you afraid of spoiling the evidence, Monk? Regardless of how you set up the actual killing, bodies full of rope burns and bullet holes aren't going to look very convincing, no matter how you plant them."

He said, "Hell, you know better than that. I remember a case where a man was found shot in a hotel room without a gun anywhere near him. Absolutely no firearm within blocks. But he'd lost a lot of money that wasn't his and written his wife a despondent letter, and the police called it suicide anyway, as I'd figured they would. Set it up right, and they'll believe what they want to believe, and to hell with the so-called clues. I've set this one up right, believe me. All that's required is the bodies." He looked down at me. "Anything I can do for you, friend? A drink, a smoke, a pillow for your head? Always happy to oblige."

He really meant it. He'd won; he could afford to be generous. Well, it was nice dealing with someone who felt no need to slug and spit in the hour of victory.

I said, "Well, I could use a nice sharp knife."

He laughed. "Good old Eric. It's a long way from Hofbaden, isn't it?"

I grinned. "It's also a pretty long way from Honolulu, amigo. You aren't there yet."

"That's right, keep the old courage up," he said cheerfully. "I'll see you in the morning, early. Sleep well."

I tried to settle myself comfortably on the hard floor.

After I'd achieved the best compromise possible, I heard Mr. Soo's voice, puzzled, from the growing darkness beside me.

"He speaks like a friend."

I said, "Friend, enemy, what the hell? He's hated me a long time. He's feeling nostalgic; he's going to be a little sorry to end all those fine years of hatred by killing me tomorrow. It will leave a hole in his life until he finds somebody new to hate, and he knows it."

Mr. Soo said softly, "Incomprehensible people!"

I said, "Hell, you folks would be lost if you couldn't shake your fists at the U.S. twice a day. You ought to know what I mean."

Mr. Soo said, "I will not discuss politics. I suppose you have no clever plan for escaping tonight."

"No," I said. "Do you?"

"Unfortunately not. I will sleep. Good night, sir."

"Good night, Mr. Soo."

He said, "My name is not Soo. No matter. Soo, for purposes of reference, will suffice. Good night."

They didn't give us much sleep. Monk had trained them well. They came in almost every hour with flashlights to check the ropes. Even so, I managed to doze off between inspections. But suddenly I found myself wide awake and sweating, although there was no man bending over me. Something had changed. The trade winds weren't blowing any longer.

Particularly on the windward side of those islands, you get so used to the steady murmur of the wind—even in a few days—that when the trees fall silent and the little breezes stop, you look around uneasily, expecting something terrible to happen, and of course it does. At least so I'd been told. The temperature rises, dogs run mad in the streets, men jump out of high windows, and lovers part, never to meet again—until the trades start blowing once more.

This didn't concern me, but I was thinking of a wounded woman in a small sailboat. *Straight downwind to Kalaupapa,* I'd said, but now there was no wind.

Without the steady, driving trades it could take her days to make it, if she lasted that long. . . .

Well, there was obviously nothing I could do about it, except count her out as far as the assignment was concerned. It had been a forlorn chance, anyway. Picturing what she might be going through out there wouldn't help anybody, so I put it out of my mind, or tried.

In the morning they came for us well before daylight. It was hot and still. We were untied and led down to the inlet in the dark. Both boats had been brought out of cover and were lying against the bank, quite motionless. Soo and I were put aboard the larger one, which had a motor box in the stern, and a funny sort of propulsion unit sticking out behind the transom that looked like the sawed-off lower end of a giant outboard. I was used to the old-fashioned type of motorboat, where the power plant shared the cockpit with you and drove a propeller by means of a shaft running through the bottom of the boat, and the steering was done by a simple, old-fashioned rudder. Maybe this rig had advantages, but I wasn't seaman enough to spot what they were.

The bow of the boat was taken up by a tiny cabin. The rest was cockpit, at the forward end of which, to starboard, were the steering wheel and other controls. To port was a kind of electronic box with switches, buttons, and dials that could have been a navigating device of some kind, but I was reasonably sure it wasn't. There were seats for six people, two at the forward end of the cockpit facing forward, two back-to-back with these facing aft, and a couple more just in front of the motor compartment, facing forward again.

Mr. Soo and I were placed in these rearmost seats, and our ankles were lashed to the chair legs—if that's what they're called at sea—which were bolted to the cockpit floor. Then, since there was no space for our arms behind us, our wrists were tied in front of us with the same strong, heavy fishing line. It was a little gain. It's easier to do something about your bonds if you have them where you can look at them. Irina jumped aboard and sat down facing us, gun in hand.

"Later you will be put in the cuddy, forward," she said. "However, Monk doesn't want you to spend too much time alone. You might be bored. So for the present you'll ride out here where I can entertain you."

Monk was standing on the bank beside the other boat, a somewhat smaller and stubbier craft boasting two huge outboard motors on the transom. At least they looked enormous to me. I guess the one I remembered from boyhood must have been Ole Evinrude's little pilot model or a very near descendant. Monk was giving instructions to a couple of men. I could hear enough to know that he was arranging a rendezvous, but not enough to have any idea where it would be.

Irina looked annoyed when Monk dropped aboard our craft and immediately used his flashlight to inspect our wrists and ankles.

"I have already checked," she said sharply. "Can't you trust me to do anything right?" She caught herself, and mopped her face, and said in the humble voice I'd come to know, "I'm sorry, Monk. I didn't mean. . . This damn *kona* weather!"

He grinned. He was in a good mood. "Check and double-check is my motto, kid," he said, patting her on the shoulder. I couldn't help wondering what their relations were and how they'd spent the night, but they weren't lovers now. His touch and voice were casual and preoccupied. "Well, don't put any more holes in the specimens than you have to. Here we go."

He went down the aisle between the seats, picking his way past the clumsy-looking water skis stowed there, and paused to take off his damp Boy Scout shirt and throw it into the little cabin. He sat down behind the steering wheel. When he turned the key, things began to rumble and vibrate behind the seats to which Soo and I were tied.

A man on the bank turned us loose. Monk maneuvered us around in the narrow channel, using, I noticed, a husky lever for a throttle and three colored buttons to work the gears: apparently the boat was equipped with an electric or hydraulic shift of some kind. I watched him carefully. I mean, I'm an automobile man at heart. A fine twisty mountain road and a good sports car is my idea of traveling. After my recent experience in the Pailolo Channel, I'd resigned myself to the fact that I'd probably never be a true sailboat sailor; and I wasn't really yearning to test my motorboating abilities, but I might have to.

So I watched him closely, by the instrument lights, as he worked the boat back and forth until he had it heading out. Then he shoved the throttle lever smoothly forward. The rumbling and burbling behind me increased in volume. The trees slid past, and some grass and sand. We slipped through a final opening and Monk gave another shove to the throttle. The boat seemed to rise and level off, planing. He switched off the instrument lights, and we headed out across the glassy dark sea. I didn't spend much time looking around. If Isobel was becalmed out here somewhere, there was nothing I could do for her and certainly nothing she could do for me.

The trip was, I figured, more than three times as long as the one we'd made from Maui to Molokai, and we made it in less than a third of the time, which shows what the internal combustion engine can do for you. As the dawn broke behind us, Irina, facing into the sunrise, put on a pair of dark glasses from the pocket of the garment she was wearing this morning: a short, sleeveless muu-muu that, except for its bright colors, looked like the kind of starched smock they used to put on very little girls.

We came up on Oahu at thirty knots—or miles per hour. From the rear of the cockpit I could read the figure but I couldn't read just how the nautical speed-ometer was calibrated. The fact that there was such a thing at all was a surprise to me. It was daylight when we rounded Diamond Head. There were many more boats out than usual, I noticed, including a good many catamarans with bright sails that didn't seem to be doing very well without wind. I could see the hotel where I was still paying rent on a room and the beach where

I'd first seen Irina. Monk threw the engine into neutral, glanced at his watch, and came aft.

"Okay, get them below while I rig your towline," he snapped at the girl. "Hurry it up before somebody comes too close; it looks as if every boat in Honolulu is heading out to welcome the *Lurline*." He was feeling some strain now, and his voice showed it. "I hope you've got your bathing suit ready under that pinafore."

Irina laughed. "Really, Monk. . . ."

"Don't really-Monk me. Just get them out of sight and get overboard where you belong. And remember the instructions. I'll make one pass. Don't forget to laugh and wave at all the nice boys. We'll go right down the side of the ship and swing off to port. At a quarter of a mile, I'll hit the firing button. You let go and fall when it blows, but not before. Make it look natural, as if you were knocked right off your skis by the concussion. I'll swing around to pick you up. By the time I've got you and the rope aboard, there should be so much smoke and confusion nobody'll be paying any attention to us. . . . That's it, tie them up good, there."

Irina, lashing my ankles, gave an extra yank to the cords. She already had Soo hogtied on the other bunk in the tiny, wedge-shaped cabin. She paused in the opening to regard me for a moment; then she smiled slowly and took off her sunglasses and dropped them into the pocket of her smock. Still smiling, she reached back to unfasten the garment and, with the same graceful movement I remembered—which she was obviously remembering too—she slipped it off with her sandals and dropped it into the cabin beside me tauntingly, like a stripper parting with a strategic tassel. She stood there for a moment in her white bikini, slim and tanned and blonde and beautiful.

Monk said, "For Christ's sake, Irina, stop posing and get back here! There's a ship putting out now. . . . Yes, there she is, right on time, the *General Hughes*. Over you go. Get those skis on and give me the word."

I heard a splash. Through the open cabin door, I saw Monk return to the controls, looking back impatiently.

Then the door slammed shut, but I heard Irina's voice: "Put her in gear. . . . All right, *hit it*!"

The boat surged ahead and hesitated briefly, fighting the resistance of girl and skis; then it was up on the step and planing, but I wasn't really paying attention. I'd been waiting for a break and I'd got it. I remembered clearly telling another girl, in a different place: *There are times when a bit of broken glass can come in very handy.*

Now if the lenses of Irina's sunglasses weren't plastic, and Monk would just stay too busy to look in on me. . . .

Chapter Twenty-six

IT WAS TRICKY work. The lenses were glass, all right, but getting one out of the frame intact, and then cracking it just right to get a usable edge, wasn't easy with my wrists lashed together. The motion of the boat didn't help, and there was always the possibility that Monk would stick his head in at any moment. He didn't even have to open the door to do it.

As usual with those small-cabin entrances, there was a sliding hatch above to give light and headroom in the doorway, and to save you from having to crawl in on hands and knees. With the hatch pulled aft to meet the upper edge of the closed door, protection would have been complete, but with the hatch shoved forward as it was, the rear end of the cabin was open to the sky. All Monk had to do was lean over from his helmsman's chair and look down.

Fortunately, he didn't, in the time it took me to prepare my cutting implement and look around for a way to hold it securely. I glanced at Mr. Soo. He'd been watching, of course, and he nodded when I showed him the half-moon of glass. We had to squirm around a bit on our bunks to get into position, but it was a cozy little place and a lot of reach wasn't needed. Soo took the glass carefully. I saw the question in his eyes. The first man cut free, of course, had all the advantages.

Mr. Soo didn't say anything. He was a realist. There was an armed man in the cockpit, and dealing with armed men was my specialty, not his. He wasn't silly enough to try to extract any meaningless promises. He just braced his hands against the edge of the cockpit to steady the improvised knife. The fact that they'd used fishline helped. Cutting through heavy rope would have taken much longer. At that, we shattered two lens-halves and had to go to a third before the strong cord parted.

I rolled back on my bunk to clear my wrists of the multiple loops Irina had used to tie me. I was barely in time. I heard Monk swear out there, and the boat swerved; then the door was flung open and he was standing there with his shiny gun in his left hand—the right was reaching out to one side to hold the steering wheel. His face was pale and furious. At first I thought he had spotted the cut cords; then I realized that his mind was on something altogether different.

"You bastard!" he said. "How did you do it, Eric? How'd you get word to them? She's turning! The damn ship's turning, do you understand? She's been recalled to harbor. How'd you do it?" The gun steadied. "Aren't you going to grin triumphantly, you cocky bastard? I'll give you one last grin, friend. Just one!"

There was no hope of jumping him. I still had yards of twine firmly wound around my wrists, not to mention the stuff on my ankles. I just looked up at him and told myself that Isobel had made it. Somehow, in spite of wounds and weather, the damn woman had made it. She'd got the word through. She was wasting her time on the cocktail circuit; she should have been an agent. She was doing a hell of a lot better than some.

I stared at the stainless steel revolver and watched the finger take up the slack of the trigger; then the muzzle dropped and Monk laughed, a short, harsh bark of sound.

"Okay, Eric. One point for you. It was the woman, wasn't it? I should have known better than to take Irina's word for it. These one-shot kids, when will they learn to finish off their cripples? But don't look so damn smug. Nothing's changed. We'll just take the *Hughes* coming in, instead of going out." He rammed the pistol back under his belt. "Just lie back and listen to the fireworks, friend."

He slammed the door shut and disappeared from sight. I hurried to clear the stuff off my wrists and got to work on my ankles, but here the fishline was against me: the little knot was tougher to solve than a big one would have been. Irina had set it up good and hard. I was thinking desperately of trying the glass once more, when my fingernails finally found the right purchase and the knot came apart. A few seconds later my legs were free.

I saw Soo looking hopefully my way, and I gave him a big friendly smile, no more. It was going to be rough enough dealing with the Monk without an unknown quantity at my back. I lay there trying to judge what was going on outside. I had a feeling we had other seagoing traffic around us: there were frequent bounces when we hit what I took to be the wakes of other boats.

Then there was a straight run and a gradual left swing, and suddenly the ship was above us, sliding past at high speed. I could see the gray side through the open hatch, and even faces looking down from the decks above. I thought I could hear masculine hoots and whistles, but the speedboat's exhaust echoed noisily from the ship's side, drowning out the other sounds.

I sensed a movement up there, and lay back, and saw Monk reach across to the electronic console to port before I realized what he was about. I'd thought he was just going to check on us in the cabin. I braced myself for noise and concussion, but there was only a click, faintly audible above the sound of the boat's progress.

Mr. Soo said calmly, "That was the ready switch, Mr. Helm. Circuits are now active. Red light is on. Charges will explode when firing button is depressed."

"What's the maximum range of your machine?"

"Approximately one mile as now set. It will operate to ten miles or farther, but the responding circuits would have had to be so sensitive that they might have been activated prematurely by stray electronic transmissions, say from the ship's own radar."

The ship was gone. I started counting seconds. Monk had said he'd fire at a quarter-mile. With the ship going one way and the boat the other, the speed of separation was somewhere around forty miles per hour, depending on the angle. Say a minute and a half, or ninety seconds, for a mile: that was a little over twenty for the quarter. I didn't dare cut it too close. I went out of there at fifteen.

I was early. He was still in his seat with both hands on the wheel, but my luck was in. For the moment he was looking back at the ship or Irina, I couldn't tell which. The ship was back there all right, receding fast, and so was the girl: a slim bronzed figure in her scanty white suit, riding her skis gracefully in the speedboat's wake.

I didn't take it all in; it was no time to be admiring the view. Monk was turning, but I managed to clip him once and yank him from the seat and, bracing myself against the cabin, kick him aft, away from the firing box at my right elbow, on which a red light now glowed. I didn't follow him all the way. There were things to be done first, and I gave a twist to the steering wheel with my left hand to send the boat straight out to sea. I glanced at the instrument board on my right. There were too many switches and dials. I knew I didn't dare monkey with them until we were well out of firing range; I might set up the wrong combination.

Monk crouched there for a moment, partially dazed; then he came around with a gun in his hand, but I was ready for him, and I kicked, and the gun went flying over the side.

He showed his teeth in a smile. "Just like old times, eh, Eric? That time you wore me down with your dancing around and long-range jabbing. Just try that here, friend."

He was right, of course. Here the advantage was all on his side. There was no place in the cramped cockpit full of bolted-down seats for any fancy footwork, and my longer reach wasn't going to be much help, either. Monk lowered his head and came for me. I just waited for him. There was nothing else to do. I was Horatius at the bridge; I had to stay between him and that glowing red light. Grudge fight or no, I knew him well enough to know that he'd break off in a minute and dive for the firing button if I gave him an opening.

So I just stood there and let him come to me and we tried a few tricks, for a starter, with the edge of the hand and the stiff fingers, and they didn't work. We both knew all the tricks, and time was running out for him. The ship was nearing the harbor again, and we were heading the other way at a good clip, running straight out to sea. He might still be able to fire if he hit it now. If not, he might still be able to swing around and close to firing range, if he got rid of me. But he had to do it fast.

He moved in with the fists to overwhelm me. I blocked some blows and took some and managed to hold my place in the aisle. He glanced around frantically and came in swinging once more with all the power of his big arms and gorilla shoulders, and I weathered that attack, too, but just barely. I looked past him.

"Your girlfriend's gone," I said. "She's lost the rope."

He grinned breathlessly. "An oldie, friend. Oh, what an oldie!"

I shrugged. As a matter of fact, I was telling the truth. Behind the boat was only the wooden bar of the tow-rope, dancing along the water. Far back I could see the floating skis and the girl's head. Monk threw a quick glance over his shoulder and saw them, too. Maybe there had been something between them, after all: he rushed me hard once more, this time trying to reach the boat's controls, to steer back there.

In his haste, he slipped and went to one knee, and I brought my knee up under his chin and, using the seats for leverage, kicked him back once more to the rear of the cockpit. That gave me a moment to examine the control board again. I prayed that Mr. Soo's one-mile range was an optimistic estimate and moved one switch from ON to OFF. There were no spectacular displays of pyrotechnics in the direction of the harbor. The red light just went out.

I heard Monk's hoarse cry and looked in his direction. He was bringing his hand out of his pants pocket with a gun that looked very familiar: not one of the fancy stainless-steel jobs that had been brandished so frequently in this business, just a plain old workaday blue weapon with a shrouded hammer. I remember Irina tossing it to him at the time of my capture. Whether he'd simply forgotten that he was carrying it—it seemed to be an easy gun to forget—or whether he'd just wanted to take me barehanded, there was no telling. He had it now.

He pointed it at me. The circuits were off, I hoped; I could risk leaving my post. I moved in on him, and threw my arm across my eyes as he fired, not knowing just what was going to come out of the gimmicked weapon. I heard two sharp little cracks like those of a kid's cap pistol, as he pulled the trigger twice. He tried a third time and the gun blew up.

I mean, it exploded like a bomb in his hand. I felt a heavy blow against my hip, and my bare chest and arm and face were sprayed with powder and scraps of hot metal. What had happened was simple enough to understand: it's as I once said, when you start playing games with firearms, nobody can predict the results.

I remembered reloading the weapon with live cartridges to deal with Pressman and switching the loads back again. But the spare-ammunition gadget holds six cartridges, and the gun only holds five. For a little while, there had been an extra live round in my pocket with the powderless ammo, and somehow I'd managed to get it into the gun. When Monk fired the first two cartridges, one or both of the bullets, with nothing but primers behind them, had stuck in the gun barrel. Then the full-charge load had fired into the blocked barrel. The pressure, with no place to go, had simply blown the weapon to pieces.

I tried to take a step forward, and my leg gave way under me. I caught myself by one of the seats, and saw the Monk standing there, but he was no longer interested in me. Blood was running freely down his face and he was wiping at it vaguely with a shattered hand. . .

It was almost too easy, after all the years of hate and all the blows that had been traded. I found that my leg would hold me, if I didn't trust it too far, and I moved in and did what I had been sent here to do.

Chapter Twenty-seven

THE WOUND WASN'T too bad. Apparently the whole front end of the revolver—the barrel and part of the frame—had come flying at me, bruising and tearing things a bit but getting no substantial penetration. What really laid me out was a case of some kind of tropical dysentery I seemed to have picked up along the way.

It was a couple of weeks, therefore, before I could limp onto a plane and settle myself for the flight back to the Mainland. As we took off, I looked down at the Honolulu waterfront and the ocean, although what I expected to see down there, after two weeks, I don't know. Of course, the Monk was down there somewhere, but an anchor and twenty feet of chain were taking care of him. It's easier to explain an agent's disappearance than his dead body, particularly when you don't want to answer too many questions about his penultimate activities.

By evening I was in Washington, pretty well exhausted, sitting in a room on the second floor of a familiar building, telling the gray-haired man behind the desk the stuff I hadn't put in my official report.

"So you let the Chinese gentleman go," Mac said.

"Yes, sir," I said. "I didn't figure his detonating device was anything our boys couldn't figure out by themselves, and I owed him a little something for his co-operation."

"Your personal debts are beside the point, Eric. The man might have been able to tell us something."

"Not us," I said. "But he could certainly have told a lot of other people about Monk. I thought you wanted that hushed up, sir. It was either kill him or let him go, so I put him ashore." I shrugged. "As Monk said, there are four hundred million of them. I didn't figure one more was going to outnumber us."

"Um," Mac said. "And the girl? She was never found?"

"No, sir." I was silent for a moment, seeing again two skis floating on an empty ocean. "She was too good a swimmer to drown, and she couldn't have swum out of sight in the time she had. I did see a fin, sir, but I'm not an expert on fins. Even if it was a shark, it could have been a perfectly harmless and friendly one. On the other hand, Irina wasn't there. Just the skis."

Mac said, "You'll be interested to know that when I asked just what it was Monk had put aboard the ship, I was told that it was a security matter."

I grinned. "That's nice. We save their damn transport, and they won't tell us what we saved it from. Well, if you don't mind, sir, I think I'll go to a hotel and sleep for a week."

"Yes, of course." He waited until I'd limped to the door, and said, "Eric. In regard to this business in Asia, just what *are* your feelings on the subject?"

I laughed. "Sir, the political opinions of an agent are those required by the job at hand."

He gave me his thin smile. "Precisely. I was just making sure you hadn't forgotten. Well, don't forget to stop by the recognition room on your way out."

I was careful not to stare at him reproachfully. I mean, an order is an order and to hell with it—even if I had just crawled out of a hospital bed and flown half-way around the world.

"Yes, sir," I said, and went down to let Smitty run off his films for me.

I won't say I learned a great deal. My powers of concentration weren't at their highest peak. Having done my duty, I limped out of the projection room and started down the hall, but stopped abruptly, hearing a voice I remembered.

"I think that shiny one looks very pretty," Isobel was saying to the supply man when I came in. "I'll take that one."

She turned, hearing me, and we stood for a moment looking at each other. She was a stranger again, nicely dressed in a light summer suit, with her hair done in the smooth way I remembered. She looked polished and expensive, and it was hard to remember the exact details of what had happened on a tropical beach and by a pool in the jungle.

"Hello, Matt," she said. "You look terrible."

"I'm glad I can't say the same for you." I looked at the attractive woman in front of me, remembering how I'd seen her last. "So you made Kalaupapa in spite of the calm," I said.

"Kalaupapa?" she said. "Why should I sail fifteen miles to Kalaupapa when there was a road and a car only a couple of miles back along the shore? I was there before the wind dropped. The only trouble was, all the nice people kept telling me to rest instead of listening to me; it was almost dawn before I could get somebody to pick up a telephone." She smiled. "You're a nice person even if you are a terrible sailor, darling. I want to thank you for putting all that money in trust for Kenneth. But you shouldn't have given it all away."

"It wasn't really my money," I said. "Claire—Winnie —would have wanted her brother to have it."

"I think so. She was just prejudiced against me," Isobel said. "But she doesn't have to worry. I'm divorcing Kenneth as soon as I can. Don't look so surprised, darling. What do you think I wanted the money for? I couldn't divorce him when he was broke, could I? But now that he's all set, to hell with him." She glanced at the man behind the desk. "Well, I'd better finish my business and get out of here. I have the feel-

ing I'm intruding on realms of desperate security. . . .
Oh, you'd better wrap it. I can't very well go through the
streets carrying it in my hand."

"Yes, ma'am," the man said.

I looked at the stainless steel revolver, and at the
handsome woman in front of me. "What's that for?" I
asked.

"Why, you know I've always wanted one," she said.
"When the man upstairs asked me how he could repay
me for everything, I just asked him to give me a gun
with all the proper documents to make it legal." She
hesitated, and gave me a questioning, smiling glance.
"Oh, and he did say something about finding a man
who'd teach me how to shoot it. Are you . . . are you
the man?"

"I guess I could be," I said.

I was.

BESTSELLERS

☐	BEGGAR ON HORSEBACK—Thorpe	23091-0	1.50
☐	THE TURQUOISE—Seton	23088-0	1.95
☐	STRANGER AT WILDINGS—Brent (Pub. in England as Kirkby's Changeling)	23085-6	1.95
☐	MAKING ENDS MEET—Howar	23084-8	1.95
☐	THE LYNMARA LEGACY—Gaskin	23060-0	1.95
☐	THE TIME OF THE DRAGON—Eden	23059-7	1.95
☐	THE GOLDEN RENDEZVOUS —MacLean	23055-4	1.75
☐	TESTAMENT—Morrell	23033-3	1.95
☐	CAN YOU WAIT TIL FRIDAY?— Olson, M.D.	23022-8	1.75
☐	HARRY'S GAME—Seymour	23019-8	1.95
☐	TRADING UP—Lea	23014-7	1.95
☐	CAPTAINS AND THE KINGS—Caldwell	23069-4	2.25
☐	"I AIN'T WELL—BUT I SURE AM BETTER"—Lair	23007-4	1.75
☐	THE GOLDEN PANTHER—Thorpe	23006-6	1.50
☐	IN THE BEGINNING—Potok	22980-7	1.95
☐	DRUM—Onstott	22920-3	1.95
☐	LORD OF THE FAR ISLAND—Holt	22874-6	1.95
☐	DEVIL WATER—Seton	23633-1	2.25
☐	CSARDAS—Pearson	22885-1	1.95
☐	CIRCUS—MacLean	22875-4	1.95
☐	WINNING THROUGH INTIMIDATION —Ringer	23589-0	2.25
☐	THE POWER OF POSITIVE THINKING—Peale	23499-1	1.95
☐	VOYAGE OF THE DAMNED— Thomas & Witts	22449-X	1.75
☐	THINK AND GROW RICH—Hill	23504-1	1.95
☐	EDEN—Ellis	23543-2	1.95

Buy them at your bookstores or use this handy coupon for ordering:

FAWCETT BOOKS GROUP
P.O. Box C730, 524 Myrtle Ave., Pratt Station, Brooklyn, N.Y. 11205

Please send me the books I have checked above. Orders for less than 5
books must include 75¢ for the first book and 25¢ for each additional
book to cover mailing and handling. I enclose $_____ in check or
money order.

Name_____

Address_____

City_____ State/Zip_____

Please allow 4 to 5 weeks for delivery.